Other books you may enjoy that have been written by Jolynn Rose:

Roslander – The Island of the Merbeings
Roslanders – The Cities under the Sea
The Tales of the Merbeings Clans
The Roslanders, Pagons and Imdom Clans
Agatha and Frank – Stranded on Rosland island
Agatha and Frank – Road Trip Adventure
Agatha and Frank – Living the Dream
The Mystery of Dixie Mountain – by Lola Smith/ Jolynn Rose

AGATHA AND FRANK
EXPLORING AMERICA

JOLYNN ROSE

Order this book online at www.trafford.com
or email orders@trafford.com

Most Trafford titles are also available at major online book retailers.

Print information available on the last page.

ISBN: 978-1-4907-9070-1 (sc)
ISBN: 978-1-4907-9074-9 (e)

Trafford rev. 08/30/2018

 www.trafford.com

North America & international
toll-free: 1 888 232 4444 (USA & Canada)
fax: 812 355 4082

PROLOGUE

Agatha and Frank had been on a road trip across the northern part of the USA for the last year and a half. But now it was time to go home for a little while to visit family and friends.

They had visited and explored many places during their travels. As far as Aggie (Agatha) and Frank are concerned, traveling in their RV to see this wonderful country of ours, was the only way to go! It was fantastic waking up in the same bed every morning, and then walking out of their RV to a new place, view and new things to explore. Not knowing what they will discover in the new area. There were always so many things to see and do during their travels.

One thing they enjoyed was going to small towns and exploring their courthouse and their back streets. That's where they find out about the history of the area they were visiting. There were many towns that they had visited; they could tell at one time they had been thriving communities. But now the towns were just hanging on by the skin of their teeth to keep their little town alive. But the towns were slowly dying.

They loved to walk on the back streets of these towns; they would see the old buildings and learn a little more about the history that had been forgotten. The Cemeteries were another place they liked to visit; there is so much you can learn about the times gone by of an area.

They planned on getting Penelope (their RV) cleaned up and a few repairs done while they were at home. They wanted her ready so when they get their next urge to head out on a new adventure. She would be ready to go. The next adventure, they planned to go on would be the central states.

In the beginning they were having a great time visiting with their family and friends. But after a few months, the visiting slowed down, and it became the same old thing again. The weather was rainy and windy, there was flooding all around the area. The storms that came in from the gulf, made it impossible to go out sailing.

They looked at their pictures from the year before, when they were in Arizona and Nevada.

They enjoyed visiting the museums and hiking in the desert. It was mostly sunny during the day, but cold at night in most of the places they went. They were really starting to miss the warm weather. Houston weather just wasn't what it used to be, with all the rain and wind they have been having. It was time to chase the sun and explore the good old USA and "Exploring America, all the little and big secrets it has.

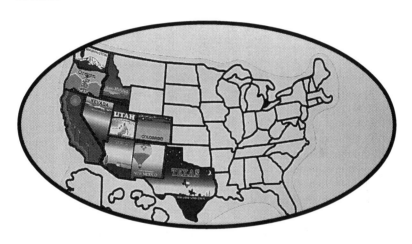

CHAPTER 1

After looking at their pictures from their earlier adventures, they started talking about all the wonderful things they have seen. It got them in the mood to do a little traveling. Aggie received a letter from Larie' today, they had met each other in Newport, Oregon and became good friends. Larie' and her husband Dean were just starting out on being full time travelers. They exchanged information and had been writing each other. They both enjoyed getting letters the old fashion way by slow mail, aka "Snail mail." Aggie hadn't heard from her in quite a while. She just assumed that Larie' was busy. But come to find out they were having a hard time of it. Aggie read the letter to Frank and this is what it said,

Hi Aggie,

It's been awhile since I wrote you but we have been pretty busy. Dean became ill right after we saw you guys in Newport, OR. We had to go inland to the VA hospital; he ended up there for a month. It took that long to figure out what was wrong with him. They found a lesion on his spinal cord. They did all kinds of test and had people from all over the country trying to understand what it was and what caused it. They also talked about removing it, but wanted to make sure it was the right thing to do. Each day he was in the hospital, he got worse. He was going numb from the waist down; his legs quit working like they were supposed to. The only way he could walk was by watching his feet and with a walker.

After three weeks they finally decided to do a treatment of massive doses of steroids for three days. On the third day Dean was able to start feeling things in his legs again. After a week they let him come home. He was supposed to recuperate for a couple weeks, but after a week he was ready to start our travels.

We decided to rent the house out to my nephew and his wife instead of leaving it empty. After loading everything into storage, we headed to my mom's property with the RV to set up our new home. We figured we could let Dean recuperate a little more before we headed off on our excursion down to the coast.

Things didn't go as planned, after about a week Dean had another episode. This time it was in his left side. I called the doctor and she said to get him into the hospital right away. They did another MRI and found another lesion on his spinal cord this time on the left side of it. That's why his left leg was causing him problems. They automatically started him on steroids again, which stopped lesion from growing. But it had already caused the damage to his nerve endings. He had lost the use of his left leg at this point. But the doctors did come to the conclusion that he has MS.

After spending three days in the hospital, he finally came back home. He couldn't use his left leg; he had to use a walker in the beginning. But the problem was he couldn't climb the steps to get into the RV, so we set him up in Mom's house. He was home for about a week when he started having complications so we went back to the doctors and they suggested that he go to rehab so they could help him with the different problems he was having. They figured he would be there for about three weeks, but Dean was determined to come home sooner if possible. He went in to the center in a wheelchair and after only two weeks he was walking again, with a cane only. He left the rehab center on his own two feet, with a little help from his cane.

It's funny to think back when he first came home the second time we got excited when he could move his big toe on his left foot and now he's walking 3 to 5 miles a day. He is such an amazing man I couldn't be prouder of him! Nothing can keep that man down!

Well I hope everything is going good for you guys. I have enjoyed your letters, it sounds like you guys have done a lot of traveling around the country, since last time we saw you. We can't wait until we can start traveling around the country. We are going to start by traveling up and down the Oregon and Washington coast. I don't know how often I'll have the Internet so I'll write when I can. I enjoy your letters and reading about your adventures, looking forward to hearing back from you.

Your friend, Larie'

After reading her letter Frank and Aggie had decided it was time to get on the road again, there was still a lot to see in Texas. Louisiana and Arkansas wasn't that far away, they could make short trips there if they wanted. Frank had a friend in Louisiana that has been asking him, when was he going to come visit him?

It was time to add a few more states to their map on Penelope. Putting the U.S. map on the side of your rig was something most people did that traveled a lot. In the travels they had seen quite a few rigs that have been completely filled up, even Canada too. Their goal was to fill up their map and hopefully go to Alaska and Canada.

They decided to just go on short trips in the beginning because the weather wasn't all that great yet. They watched the weather forecast and saw that there was going to be a week of sunshine in Louisiana and Arkansas. It was only a hop, skip and a jump to Louisiana. They loaded up Penelope their RV and the girls (dogs) and told the kids they would only be gone for a few weeks. Look out Louisiana here they come!

CHAPTER 2

On the road again

The next morning there was no fan fair; they just started up their RV and headed down the road. The plan was to go see Frank's friend Tom, an old friend from the Army, and then go up to Arkansas. Tom lives in Holly Beach, Louisiana. He lost his home to a hurricane a few years ago, but he had rebuilt.

Aggie wanted to check out Port Arthur, on their way to visit him, she had read about it earlier that week, and it sounded interesting to her. This is what she found out about the town. "Port Arthur is a city in Jefferson County within the Beaumont–Port Arthur Metropolitan Statistical Area of the U.S. state of Texas. It is located on the western bank of Sabine Lake. The Rainbow Bridge across the Neches River connects Port Arthur to Bridge City. Aurora was located near the mouth of Taylor Bayou on Sabine Lake, at the site of present-day Port Arthur. The town was conceived as early as 1837, and by 1840 promoters led by Almanzon Huston were advertising town lots. Although some lots were sold, Houston's project failed to materialize. The area came to be known as Sparks after John Sparks and his family moved to the shores of Sabine Lake near the Aurora town site."

"The Eastern Texas Railroad, completed between Sabine Pass and Beaumont just before the outbreak of the Civil War, passed about four miles west of Sparks. The railroad passing track at this point was named Aurora after the Houston project. The rails were removed during the Civil War. A few scattered settlers remained until 1886, when a destructive hurricane led residents to dismantle their homes and move to Beaumont. By 1895 Aurora was a ghost town. The abandoned community, however, soon became the site of Arthur E. Stilwell's new city, Port Arthur." To Aggie it was more interesting to go into town when she knew a little bit of the history.

As they drove into Port Arthur, they saw the old buildings from when it was a thriving town, but stood mostly empty now. As they drove to the Rainbow bridge there was more industry. The bridge was longer than most bridges they have crossed in the past. It goes across a river and then ran along the edge of Sabine Lake. When Aggie looked over at the lake, she could see on one side was Port Arthur which had all kinds of industry activity, but on the other side there was nothing. According to the sign it was a wildlife reserve.

As they drove across the bridge they could see the swampland in the distance, it was the wildlife reserve. As they left the bridge all they could see was wetlands area, with a lot of scrub brush. There were canals on both side of the road; on one side Aggie saw an alligator. Frank offered to stop, so she could check out the alligator. But Aggie had no desire to do so!

Frank has always talked about Tom and what a wonderful guy he is. Frank enjoyed talking about the good old days with Tom. Tom was an old army buddy. They had met in the early 70s when they were both assigned to 2nd Armored Division at Fort Hood, Texas. They were in the same Company but really didn't get to know each other until much later. He remembers that they both came on orders and got their clearing papers at the same time. But that his port calls (military term for orders to overseas transport) was a week later than Toms.

A lot of the guys came on levy during that time; everybody was running around processing out of the post. Frank had been to Germany five years earlier, he was levied to Germany again which wasn't any big deal to him. Frank ended up in Krabbenlock Kassern, in Ludwigsburg, Germany this time. Aggie had asked Frank to write about his time in the military, so she could put it in her book that she will be writing about their lives someday. This is the story that Frank wrote:

> Krabbenlock had been built back in the 1880s for the Kaisers horse Calvary. There was a row of four barracks, all made of stone and brick. The buildings were four stories tall; the mess hall was in a separate building that was for the whole post. The post was shaped like a square about 500 meters on each side. As it grew the city of Ludwigsburg had surrounded the post, which had houses and apartments built just across the street on all sides.

Frank left Frankfurt and the "21st Repo depot," as the GIs called it, it stands for Replacement Detachment by train headed south. He had never seen that part of West Germany before as the last time he was assigned to a Nike Herkules Missile Battery, north of Frankfurt. So this was all new for him.

As always, German trains ran like clockwork. He was given a train ticket and was told to be standing by a number track at the Frankfurt Main train station at the departure time. Minutes later, he was in route to the German state of Baden-Württemberg and the city of Stuttgart. The train stopped at many small towns and cities along the way. It took about two hours when they pulled up into the main train station and stopped. The train slowed to a crawl, and stopped at the platform on track three. Aggie thought to herself, it's hard to believe that he still remembers what track he stopped at after 40 odd years.

Anyway, the conductor walked through the train announcing that the stop was Stuttgart. Frank grabbed his duffel bag and suitcase and jumped off the train, not sure of what to do next. There were two guys there to meet him; he could tell they were obviously American soldiers, though they were dressed in civilian clothes. They had a big grin on their face and said, "Sgt. Smith, we are here to pick you up and take you to Krabbenlock, 34th Sig. Bn. The 21st Repo had called the unit earlier and told them you would need to be picked up at the BahnHoff." Their names were Craig Lowery and Dink Reynolds. They took him to the barracks where he would live for the next two years. As he was walking up the stairs he heard a familiar voice, he looked up and there stood Tom at the top of the stairs, smiling down at him. Frank asked him, "What the hell are you doing here?" Tom replied back, "I was here first, are you following me?" They both laughed and shook hands. Tom told him, after you go sign in and put up your gear. I'll show you around the place, there isn't much to see. Frank agreed, and headed up the stairs with Craig and Dink. They showed him to his bunk, and said "Welcome to your new home". It was in a large open barracks, and each soldier had a bed, foot locker and a wall locker, Frank didn't mind, what else does a man need anyway?

He put up his gear and headed out to meet Tom. Craig and Dink decided to join them besides there wasn't anything else to do. They all became good friends while he was there. Frank has always had a lot of respect for Tom. Because he had done three tours in Vietnam and was wounded once and lost a good chunk of his guts. He taught himself to play the guitar because there was nothing else to do in the hospital for six months and he never let it get him down. They tried to keep in touch through the years, but like most life stories they lost touch for many years. Then they accidentally ran into each other in Fort Hood, Texas. They both happened to be at the VA Hospital at the same time.

As they got closer to where Tom's old place used to be, they decided to go check it out. They had heard that there wasn't much left of it. They weren't around when it happened. They were stranded on Rosland Island, at that time.

As they pulled up to where the house used to be it was horrible to see all the damage. Where there were once a dozen houses or so, now there wasn't even one house. Only the pipes were coming out of the piles of dirt and cement. There were huge cement slabs that were now being used as jetties to protect the rest of the land in the area. At one time it was a beautiful place with the beach that went on for miles, but now with all the devastation all you could see was the disaster left behind.

After they had looked around and walked down the beach for a while it was time to go. They loaded up the girls (dogs) and headed to Holly beach. This is where most of the people rebuilt their homes. As they pulled into Holly beach they could tell that the locals took extra measures to make sure their homes were safe from another hurricane. Their houses were on stilts a good floor and a half up in the air. They also built a very large barer to protect them from the ocean. It was made out of sand, rock and cement it stood between them and the ocean.

As they pulled up to Tom's house, Tom and his wife came out to greet them. Tom pointed at where they should park the RV. Frank pulled in right next to the house; it was a great little parking space with all the amenities.

There were hugs all around! Susie told them that they better be hungry because she made a lot of food. She and Tom went out fishing this morning to get some fresh fish for the barbecue.

It was great to see them both; it had been a long time. Last time they saw them is when their kids had the welcome home party. After being stranded on Rosland island for 5 ½ years, and that has been four years ago. They had a lot of catching up to do!

Tom and Susie showed them around the new house. The hurricanes are still bad but at least they don't get the full force of the storms anymore. There have been a couple of hurricanes come though in the last few years, but so far everything has worked out just fine.

They had such a great outlook about things, when the water surrounds them. Tom says he doesn't have to leave his house to go fishing and has gotten a few new chairs and other items from the storms, as if the storm is saying sorry for the inconvenience. Things just float in, sometimes it will be the neighbor's furniture and other times they have no clue where it comes from. The water never stays very long, so it's no big deal!

Suzie wasn't kidding when she said she made a lot of food! They could eat leftovers for the next two days while they were there. "Great food and good company make life worth living," Suzie said. Frank and Tom were busy talking about the good old days. Aggie and Suzie decided to take the dogs and walk around town. Suzie fell in love with the girls; she kept picking up Sheba and giving her hugs. Sheba had no problem with that, she liked being carried.

It seemed strange to Aggie to walk underneath somebody's house, all of the houses were on stilts. Some of the houses were very colorful; one was a really bright egg yolk yellow, the other ones were a variety of colors; baby blue, pink and light yellow. They walked around the neighborhood and Susie told her about the different neighbors and what they did for a living. Most of them were retired, some were semi retired fishermen.

The next couple of days were great for the guys. They got to reminisce about the good old days in Germany and went fishing in the morning. When they came back they had a half dozen fish, and were hungry. They put some of the fish on the Barbie, and the rest in a bucket to marinate for smoking later.

The ladies just hung out, enjoying the sun. They went for a walk on the beach where they found a long stem red rose, with only a few pedals have fallen off it, which was weird Right? Then they continued to walk and found four more a few feet away, in a pile, just lying on the beach. Aggie picked one up, there was a pedal missing but the bloom itself was as beautiful as if it was just laid there. Aggie told Suzie, I guess maybe someone was proposed to, and was turned down. Suzie had another idea, she said, "Maybe someone was cremated and the ashes were laid to rest here and the flowers were their goodbyes. As they continue to walk they found a sixth rose again lying on the beach, you have to wonder why the roses were there. Aggie told Suzie, I guess we'll never know.

They continued with their walk, when they noticed a couple of men had wadded out fishing. When all of a sudden they turned and started running out of the water with their poles in the air, as if something was after them.

Aggie and Susie wasn't sure what was going on but they were going to watch and see what happened. Suzie said, "Maybe there's a shark after them!" Aggie responded could be, one thing about the beach there's always something going on. The guys finally reached the edge of the water and turned and started pulling their line in. The one guy pulled up a stingray; it was about 3 feet wide on the end of his line. After standing there for a little while they decided to release it back into the ocean. He flipped the stingray onto its back and pulled out the hook and flipped it back over and pushed it back toward the ocean. They didn't have to tell it twice it swam off into the water, hopefully never to be caught again.

They took one trip to the wildlife reserve where they found a hiking trail, which led into the reserve. It had a sign posted, "Beware of alligators," They kept the dogs on leashes and close to them. There was a canal on each side of the path, as they looked into one of the canals they spotted a few alligators, sunbathing on the bank. They kept an eye out for the alligators after that. The grass along the edge of the path is very short on each side but after about 3 feet it became very long; it wouldn't have taken too much for the alligators to hide in it. They were sure there was an alligator in wait, just waiting for the dogs to get close enough for them to grab.

They stopped and talked to one of the hikers and he told them that this was a great place to bird watch. He started telling them all about the different birds that were in the area. It was surprising how many birds lived in the area.

They walked back to the picnic area to have their lunch. As they crossed the bridge they looked down into the canal, where they saw an alligator waiting to be fed. The bridge was about 6 foot higher than the alligator, so they felt safe. They didn't think it could climb up the ditch. Well they were hoping anyway. Aggie figured it was waiting for the leftovers, she was also pretty sure it wasn't the first time he waited for leftovers. But there was a sign that said, "Do not feed the alligators!" The guys wanted to feed it, but the ladies told them "No!" After they had their lunch they loaded up the car and headed back to Holly Beach. It turned out to be a beautiful sunny day in Louisiana.

That evening Tom and Susie had friends come over and they all played cards. Frank and Aggie always enjoyed meeting new people and hearing the stories about their adventures. These people had a lot to talk about between the hurricanes and their fishing trips. There was always something going on around there. They were all so upbeat and fun to be with.

The next morning they got up late because they didn't get to bed until around three. What a great evening! But it was time to head back home. It was great visiting with them and catching up on all the things that have been going on in their lives, with the promise of keeping in touch they headed back to Texas. It had only been a week, but the kids acted like they had been gone for months. Aggie told Wanda, I guess we should go away more often! Wanda just smiled and didn't say a word.

It didn't take long before they planned their next trip, they knew of a couple of Thousand Trails Resort campgrounds up north they wanted to check out. They were so glad they had invested in this resort so many years ago.

CHAPTER 3

Lake Tawakoni, TX

After two weeks they are ready to travel and this time they were going to Lake Tawakoni, it wasn't far from Houston. According to the brochure, it has a 200 mile shoreline, and has a variety of fish; Catfish, Striped and Hybrid Striped Bass, White Bass and Largemouth Bass. In 1995, the Texas legislature declared Wills Point the bluebird capital of Texas.

Aggie was looking forward to going on the road again even if it was just for a week or two. It didn't take much for her to get cabin fever. She had received another letter from Larie', it sounded like they were having a great time.

Hello there!

It was good talking to you the other night; I hope we can get down to Texas next year. Well we made it to Long Beach, WA Thousand Trails Resort a week ago. We have been exploring the area; there is a walking path not far from where we have set up camp, it is about 500 feet from us. It runs along the coastline quite a ways. It sounds like you're ready to do some more traveling, hopefully this summer we can meet somewhere! As per your request I'll add history about the places we go explore in my letters.

The path we discovered is really nice! It is paved and goes for 8.5 miles along the coastline, it's called Discovery Trail. "It connects Long Beach and Ilwaco, its big enough for pedestrians and bicyclists to travel on in comfort. According to the signs, "The trail follows William Clark's (of Lewis and Clark) ocean side hike and it is dotted with interpretive signs, historical art and vantage points to see the ocean and the surrounding area. According to the brochure modern day explorers can search for the hundred plus geographies hidden up and down the peninsula." I guess we'll find out.

To our delight they were having a car show in Long Beach over the weekend, it is called Rod Run. There were hundreds of old cars of all kinds. It was quite amazing there were cars cruising up and down the main drag of town each evening. We even got into the traffic a few times and just waved at people as we drove by. During the day they would park their cars all over town, so people could check them out. It felt like a huge party, without the alcohol. Well during the day anyway!

Just in case you didn't know Long Beach is in Washington, right on the edge of the Columbia River and the Pacific Ocean. It's about 15 miles to go to Astoria, Oregon from here. The weather's been nice so we have been able to walk quite a bit. There are signs all over warning you about bears, but so far we haven't seen any. We saw a few garbage cans that looked like they had an encounter with a bear or two. We also went to the Cranberry Museum one day with my Aunt Simone; it was a lot more interesting than I thought it would be. It's amazing the process they have to gather up the berries! It is a working cranberry farm and research unit, but we visited during the off season, so there weren't any cranberries to see.

We have adopted the Discovery Trail as our hiking trail, we have been picking out a section to walk on every day, and we have been getting our 5 miles in each day. There are statues of Lewis and Clark, Sturgeon that is a good 6 foot long and many other things to look at as you walk down the path. In one section there's even a boardwalk that you can take, there is a viewpoint that you can see the ocean from. Otherwise all you see on the path is sand dunes and tall grass.

I know how much you like histories; we stopped at the Museum at Cape Disappointment and North Head. According to the brochure, "Cape Disappointment and North Head lighthouse has kept watch over the Long beach for well over a century. Known as the graveyard of the Pacific, the stench of water where the ocean meets the Columbia River has down more than 2000 ships and claimed more than 700 lives in 1700s. Cape Disappointment lighthouse has kept vigilance on the area since 1856; guiding sailors safely pass the coast. The second lighthouse, North head, was built in 1898." As we looked out over the mouth of the Columbia River it wasn't hard to understand why so many ships have sunk.

Nearby was Fort Columbia which had been turned into a museum. The museum was really well done. It displayed artifacts from the Corp's and Chinook tribal history exhibits. It also had vestiges of military life at the fort. We went out on the deck, which was on the coast side so we could see the ships coming in and going out of the Columbia River. We're getting ready to leave here and head to Seaside, Oregon and spend three weeks there. I hope to hear from you soon, and I'll keep you updated on where we're at.

Your friend, Larie

That got Agatha thinking about heading out again, but this time for a few months. Frank didn't care if they traveled or not as long as he could go fishing and relax he was good to go. Frank looked forward to fishing, and the kids had promised to come up for a day or at least the weekend. So off they went for another adventure.

They arrived at Lake Tawakoni around midday; there had been a lot of flooding in the campground. Some of it was blocked off for now, because of the flooding and landslides. The Ranger had warned them about the snakes' driven out by the water coming into the campground. He told them that they had killed a 5 foot long Copperhead just that morning; it had come into somebody's campground. He also warned us to check around the camp ground area before letting the dogs out. He said you never know when there might be a snake around.

As they drove around they could see where all of the areas that had been flooded, it looked pretty nasty. They weren't sure if they really want to stay in a park that was having so many problems. But they decided to stay for couple days just to see if it got better later on. The weather was supposed to be nice for the next week or so. Hopefully, things would dry out and the snakes would go back to their regular hangouts.

After getting set up they decided to take the dogs for a walk and check out the campground. Of course, keeping an eagle eye out for any snakes that may be around. On the ground or in the trees, they have learned earlier that snakes kinda like hanging out in trees too.

As they walked towards the lake they could see vultures hanging around on the water's edge it didn't make much sense to them but oh well vultures do what vultures do! As they got closer they could see that they were eating catfish. Frank couldn't figure out why anyone would be throwing out catfish.

As they continued on their walk they could see how far the water had come up during the flooding. Where you normally would park a RV, there was water, the electrical poles were in the middle of the water. As they walked over the bridge they saw something floating in the water. It was a large dead snake, and must have been the one that the Ranger had killed earlier that day.

Aggie wanted Frank to pull the snake out of the water, so she could take a picture of it. But they couldn't find anything that would reach it; they gave up and continued on their walk. Aggie told Frank maybe we'll see a live one while here. Frank told her as long as it's at a safe distance I have no problem with that.

The campground also had three smaller ponds, which were filled with frogs, turtles and water moccasins. The Ranger had warned them about the water moccasins earlier that day. They didn't see any but they were pretty sure they were out there. They did see the turtle's heads and a few sunbathing out on the edge of the pond. And on the other side the frogs were just sitting out, about a twenty of them, it was really interesting to see. One thing about Texas they have a lot of frogs and turtles around.

Each day they would walk a different direction, to see what they could discover. Over by the Lodge there were two geese and three ducks, two were Mallard and one was white, and they all hung out together. Every time Frank and Agatha got close to them the two geese would put their heads down and act like they were going to attack them. It was as if they were protecting their duck friends, this happened every time that they walked in that area.

Another area of the campground was pretty much flooded every time it rained and after a day of dry weather, the water would be gone. They would walk to the water's edge and see dead catfish everywhere. I guess that meant that the water receded very quickly, so the catfish couldn't swim away. Now they understood why there were so many catfish on the ground. What a great deal for the vultures.

They decided to go for a longer walk today; they went to the far side of the campground. They hadn't made it over there yet, because they never knew what the weather was going to be like in the next 15 minutes. But it was supposed to be a sunny day all day, so they took the girls with them.

It was a nice area; it had another lodge and a playground for kids. But the camping spaces were still flooded from the earlier rainstorms. As they were walking the dogs in the camping area, they spotted a dog over by one of the trailers, and it wasn't tied up. It was crouching down as if it was going to pounce. They decided to turn around and head back towards the Lodge.

They kept an eye on the dog and continued to walk away from it. They observe the dog was still following them. It looked like a pit bull mix, dark brown and black, that's all they really could tell about it. They weren't sure what the dog was going to do, because it kept crouching down and watching them.

Aggie kept looking back and she finally picked up Sheba and told Frank to pick up Susie just in case the dog attacks. It had happened before in Idaho and they were not going to take any chances with their dogs. The dog continued to follow them. Frank picked up some rocks and started throwing them at the dog, not trying to hit it, but to scare them away. It stayed at bay but continued to follow them.

They walked a little faster and continued to watch the dog; they made it to the Ranger's office, which was about a block and a half away. They went into the Ranger's office and told him about the dog. The Ranger looked out the door and told them, "That's

Bella she wouldn't hurt a fly! She's been around here for two years, somebody left her here as a puppy and she just made it her home. She's kind of the campground mascot." That didn't make them feel any better so they carry the dogs until they didn't see Bella anymore. Bella stayed underneath the ranges truck, but they could feel her eyes watching them. But that wasn't the end of the story.

The next morning when Aggie and Frank went out for their walk with the girls, there was Bella. Susi always barks inside the RV when it was time to go for their morning walk. This is important to know, this is how Bella knew they would be coming out of the RV.

She then would follow them around as they walked around the campground. Never getting close but always keeping an eye on them. Then the day came she decided it was time to make friends with them. Aggie thinks it's all the hot dogs she gave her, but Frank felt it was because she liked Susie. As Bella walked up to the dogs, with her tail waggling, they were pretty sure that she wasn't going to hurt them.

For the next couple of days this is the way it went. Bella would cross the large field that was between them and where she hung out at night. Once she heard Susie bark, she would come running across the field. It was the funniest thing; she would greet Susie and act like we weren't there. Susie and she became great friends for the next week. Every time they came out of the RV Bella would run across the field and join them in their walk and to play with Susie. Before the week was out there was a nice path where Bella would cross the field. Aggie would look out the window and watch her come bounding across the field to hang out with them. Sheba really didn't care for her; she was a little too big for her liking.

As Frank and Agatha would walk around the park they would run into people that knew Bella and said she was a sweetie but she wouldn't let them pet her. She would take food, but that was it. Aggie didn't tell them that she had been petting her for the last couple of days.

They were getting ready to go to their next campsite when they became aware that Bella had disappeared! It worried them so they walked over to where they first saw her, and there she was. She came over to say Hi and then went back to her home. Aggie was happy to know she did have a home after all.

It turned out to be a nice campground, after the flood waters receded. With the weather being nice for a week, they were able to mow the field and clean up the campsites. There wasn't much to do there, because it was winter. It still filled up on the weekends and the holidays, a lot of people came to go fishing and boating. The next site wasn't that far, they were going to Lake Texoma.

CHAPTER 4

Laundromats

Before they headed out to Texoma they wanted to get the laundry done. There is normally a Laundromat at the campgrounds so they decided to go there to get it done. One thing Aggie liked about the Laundromat at this one, it takes credit cards, and that made it nice if you didn't have any quarters. Otherwise, they would have to go find some place to get the quarters. It could be a challenge sometimes, because the store could be closed or there was no place around to get quarters.

As they walked into the Laundromat with their clothes, they saw a sign saying, "The network was down," which meant they could only use quarters. Of course, they didn't have any quarters with them and the store that they would normally go to get quarters was closed.

They loaded up the laundry and decided to head in to town to get the laundry done. The town was about 20 miles away so they decided that they would have dinner there, after they finish their laundry. They walked into the Laundromat and headed to the change machine to get their quarters. Frank saw a sign that read, "Tens, five or one dollar bills only." Which of course, they only had a $20 bill, and there was no place around to break a 20. Frank guessed it isn't a good thing to do laundry on Sunday. Most of the businesses are closed in the small towns on Sunday. They loaded up their laundry, and decided to wait until they could break the 20.

Aggie asked Frank how many Laundromats you think we have been in since we started this adventure. Frank replied, "I have no clue but it's been a lot!"

Laundromat buildings are the unsung hero of our country. At one time the Laundromat was the place to go. It was a weekend activity with the family. In Aggies's family, Mom would load up the laundry and the kids and go to town. Once the laundry was put into the washer, they would walk down to the local grocery store and each would get a candy bar. Her Mom would say it was payment for their hard work. Aggie figured it was her way of making them feel good about being there to help her. We kids really never wanted to go with her but we had no choice she needed the help. As Aggie got older, she figured it was because dad wanted a break from everyone!

Aggie really never did much; her older sister Jill helped the most. They never liked the way Aggie folded the clothes. Aggie said it was her way of getting out of work. She hated doing laundry; if she had it her way she would throw the clothes away once they were dirty. She always thought wouldn't it be nice if they were made out of paper. Then you could roll it up and use it for the fire. Now here she is asking her husband about how many Laundromat's they have been to. Pay back is a bitch, as she always said. Then Aggie asked him which is the most memorable one that they have been to?

Frank replied, "I would have to say it was Benson, Arizona. Remember how run down the building was and behind the building was all kinds of broken machines, washers and dryers. The area was in a pretty run down part of the town. There were little shacks everywhere! Isn't that the place where you found the extra laundry in with ours? I think it was." Aggie replied, yes it was! I couldn't believe it, when I started pulling out ours; I found somebody else's in with it. I could have sworn that the washer was empty. I wonder if they ever came back looking for it? Frank replied, well it was double clean if they did! The next place had to be Vegas, it was nice inside, but there were homeless guys everywhere outside. Aggie told Frank, it wasn't that they were homeless; it was the way they looked at us. Frank replied back,

"True, the one guy acted like he was going to attack us if we got any closer to him." I guess it was the growling that had me backing away. What was the nicest one? Aggie asked. Frank replied, "I would have to say the one in Deming, New Mexico, it was clean and had lots of machines to choose from.

There was a small town by the campground they were staying in, but they never saw any Laundromats there. So they stopped at the coffee shop and asked if there were any Laundromats in town. The lady said, "Of course, just behind this building there is one, it's a pretty nice one to! Frank and Aggie looked at each other and shook their heads. Aggie turned to the lady and asked if she could break a 20 for them. She said, "Of course!" They drove around back and sure enough there was a large Laundromat. It catered to the RV Park that was there and the townspeople. After three long hours of sitting there waiting for the laundry to get done they headed home.

The girls were happy to see them, as they entered the RV with the laundry. They put the laundry down on the couch and hooked up the dogs and took them him out for a walk. Three hours is a long time to be sitting inside and not being able to go to the bathroom. The girls made it very clear they wanted to go outside. Sure enough within the first three minutes they were finishing their business, and then it was time for them to run around and have some fun. This is pretty much the routine every time they go to do the laundry.

They finally got the laundry put up and started packing up for the next trip. Lake Texoma wasn't that far away so they figured they would leave around midday. But after seeing the weather forecast they decided to leave earlier because there was a serious storm coming in by 11:00 AM tomorrow. It was hard to believe since it was such a beautiful sunny warm day. But that's Texas for you! There can be three different types of weather in a short amount of time. They finished packing up all the things outside and broke down everything inside that they could. All they had to do is pull out tomorrow morning early.

CHAPTER 5

Lake Texoma here we come

When they woke up the next morning it was a beautiful sunny day. It was hard to believe that there was a serious rain storm coming in. When they watched the weather forecast in the morning, they said the storm was coming earlier than they originally thought. They were glad they are ready to head out and hopefully beat the storm. As usual it didn't work out that way. Once they got on the freeway they could see the dark black clouds coming straight on. They could see the sheets of water coming out of the clouds; it was so thick it looked gray.

It looks like they were going to run right into the storm. After about 30 minutes on the road, the rain started coming down lightly at first. But it didn't take long for it to become a monsoon. Aggie was glad that she was driving behind Frank; at least it wasn't hitting her full force.

Aggie couldn't get over the idiots that were passing her going at least 70 miles an hour. She had to wonder what was wrong with these people. Then the truckers would go by and drowned the car. It took everything she could to see the road. If it wasn't for the RV being in front of her it would have been almost impossible to see the road. At least Frank was high enough up that he wasn't getting the splash from the idiots that were going by. This is always been a pet peeve of Aggie, why can't people use common sense when the weather is bad!

As she looked off to the right she could see the clear blue skies in the distance. If only they could get to the turn, so they could head east. She finally did see a sign that told her they only had 10 more miles before they reached the turn off and drive out of the storm.

It was like someone had turned off the water as soon as they made their turn and drove for about 3 miles and it was sunny again. She radioed Frank and told him to drive like crazy, so they would stay in front of the storm. He replied back, Roger that!

They arrived at the new campground and the weather was beautiful there hadn't been any rain at all there. The Ranger told them that they usually miss a lot of the bad weather, because of the lakes and where they are located at. That was music to Frank and Aggies ears. They were getting pretty tired of all these rainstorms and were looking forward to some sunny days.

They found themselves a nice location away from everyone; it was a corner space and must have been used as a leased spot at one time. The woods were behind them and the resort cabins that they rented out were a stone throw away. The only bad thing about it was there was a funny smell. It was a strong chemical smell. Frank called the Ranger station to ask them about the smell. The Ranger told him that they had just sprayed to kill the weeds. The Ranger told them the smell should be gone within the next 30 minutes or so. That was good news to them; at least they won't have to smell it the whole time they were there.

They were unloading the rigs; Aggie was working on emptying the Jeep. She went to close the back tailgate, as she was shutting it there was a loud explosion. The back window shattered, it didn't hit anything, it just exploded. She called to Frank to come check it out. It just happened that one of the Park Ranger happened to be passing by when the window exploded.

The first thing Frank did was ask her, what did you do? Aggie replied I didn't do anything; I was just shutting the tailgate, and I didn't even slam it hard. The Ranger offered his opinion and told them, it's pretty hot out. The difference in temperature from where you were at to here is quite a difference.

Aggies responded yeah that's it, I know I didn't hit anything! Frank just shook his head, and walked back to the RV. Aggie called to him and told him well at least the insurance will pay for it! Frank turned and smiled, and told her I guess you better call them. Make sure you take some pictures just in case they want them. Aggie thought to herself, of course I will! But figured she shouldn't say it out loud, Frank didn't look too happy.

Aggie picked up the bigger pieces and went into the RV to get a broom and dust pan to clean up the rest. While she was in the RV she made the phone call to the insurance company. They gave her a number to call and set up an appointment to have someone come out to fix the back window. Because they needed to have the person out to the campsite, it was going to take four days before they could be there.

Aggie explained to Frank what was going on and he told her he would cover the back window with a tarp. So the rain wouldn't get into the Jeep. He grabbed the small tarp and some gorilla tape and went to it. When he was done there was no way the rain was going to get in to the Jeep. They had to drive into town later that day and you couldn't tell the glass was missing, because the tarp was good and tight. Aggie thought to herself, that's my man anything that needs to be wrapped up, covered up, or packed, he's the guy to do it.

They spent the rest of the day exploring the new campground and setting up camp. The campground was huge, one of the bigger campground that they had been to. At least this one hadn't been flooded on a regular basis, like the others. They were only 6 miles from Oklahoma and the plan was to drive up and run around Oklahoma, just to see what was up there.

The campground was pretty quiet during the week because of the lack of people, but when the weekend came it filled up pretty quickly. Where they had parked the RV, there were cabins not too far away from them. They filled up pretty quick for the weekend, because they were reserved by a church group. It was for all single moms and their children. They came for the weekend to have some fun. By the sounds of it they were having a lot of fun!

One of their day adventures was to head up to Oklahoma. They went over the Red River into Oklahoma. They drove around on the back roads into the little towns that they came to. It was always interesting to see what the little town history was. They discovered early on that small towns in each state have different types of culture and were built for a variety of reasons at that point in time.

They reached the freeway and crossed over to head back home. When they discovered the Win Star casino, it ran along the freeway for miles. They had seen advertisements on TV, but had no clue it was so close to where they were staying.

It was quite an amazing place; each connecting building was set up for different parts of the world. They stopped to try their hand at some slots; it didn't take them long to go through $40. So they went to have lunch at Toby Keith bar. It was an interesting place; they played Toby Keith music videos and had all kinds of items on the wall from different country singers. After they ate it was time to head for home.

When they got home Aggie checked her gmail and she had received another letter from Larie. She enjoyed getting letters from her, there was always something going on with them.

Hello Aggie,

It's been an interesting month. In my last letter I told you that we were going to Seaside which we did. The weather here is still pretty bad we had a couple clear days, but most of the time it's been raining and really windy. A tornado hit Manzanita which is about 20 miles from where we are located, and then another one hit in Washington, not far from Long Beach, where we just came from.

The winds have been in the 60s and 70s miles an hour, off and on for the last week. We lost our awning during the last wind storm. It was pretty wild to see. We were sitting in the RV and all of a sudden the awning flew up over the top of the RV and then came back down with a bang against the RV. Then there was no wind again, just one little gust, and it was all over. One of the awning arms broke off from the RV, it just hung down on the side of the RV, with only one side connected to it. The funny part about it was Dean was just in the process of putting his shoes on to go out and put it up before the winds came. The weather forecast was for high winds later on in the afternoon. It was just a short burst of wind and then it was gone. Well I don't know if it's funny, but it's always something.

With all the rain, the RV was surrounded with about 2 inches of water except for a small path, which we could walk to the Jeep. The water just came and went on a regular basis, it really counted on how much rain we had that day.

Our neighbors had quite the unpleasant incident going on at their place last night. We were lying in bed when we heard a dog yike, and then the neighbors yelling at their dog to come here, and then the smell! We looked out the window and saw them holding a towel around the dog. We were really glad that we had the window shut, even though we could still smell it a little bit, Skunk!

The next day we talked to the neighbors and they said their dog went up against a skunk. They had two Cocker Spaniels, only one of them had gotten sprayed by the skunk. The other one I guess was smart enough to stay away. Bill the guy that owned the dogs said that he couldn't believe how hard it was to find tomato juice that late at night. He had to go to a couple different stores before he had enough to wash the stink away from the dog. He said that the RV still smelled but not as bad as it did before. Dean told me we are not letting the dogs out at night without being on leash. We sure in the hell, didn't want to have the dogs get sprayed by a skunk. Of course I have to agree with him.

The tide has been up and some of the access to the beaches has been closed because of all the storms. So we really haven't done much walking. But the one time that we decided to go on a walk on the beach, we got the surprise of our life.

When you've been raised in Oregon one of the things you learned about the coast is to keep an eye out for sneaker waves. We decided to explore a beach we haven't been to before; it was a state park. It had a nice little path that went down to the beach. We could tell that there was a storm out to sea, because of the foam on the beach. The foam was pretty thick. There was only one family there, and they were in the distance and walking toward us.

We were walking to the water's edge and stopped to check out some rocks and play with the dogs. We turned our backs for only a moment. Dean caught site of a wave coming at us. He told me later, it looked like it was about a foot high, as far as he could tell. He yelled "RUN" I didn't look or question him; I took off running to the bank, pulling the dogs with me. Thank God I didn't let them off their leashes. I was ahead of Dean, and he was running as fast as he could, when the wave hit us. I went down and he was able to continue to stand and fight the water upright. As the water covered over me, Dean said he lost sight of me because of the foam and the next thing he knew a log came up over the top of me so he pushed it off. It was a guess where I was; he couldn't see me because of all the thick foam. He told me later the water had come up to his waist and he was glad he had his cane to help hold him up.

I on the other hand held on to a log that was close to me and in my other hand I had the dog's leashes. The wave swept over me the first time and Dean tried to help me out when the second wave came in and knocked me back down again. I still had the dog leashes in my hand. As the water receded back again I realized that the dogs were being pulled back into the water, under the foam. I saw a black spot floating off in the waves, it had to be Rosie. That's when I pulled the leashes and brought them back to me and about that time another wave hit me. As I laid there holding onto the leashes, the third time I got up, and the family that was down the beach was now standing on the bank looking at us. The woman yelled at her husband to help me. He reached down to help me, I grabbed Rosie and instead of reaching out to grab his hand I handed him Rosie. Peppy was already on the bank, thank goodness. The man looked at me kind of funny, but took Rosie anyway.

Dean was standing by my side as he helped me up, we turned and the water was way back where it originally started, which was about 30 feet away. We're not really sure how big the waves were because we were kind of busy and all of that happened in a matter of minutes. But we still don't like getting too close to the water. If you ever on the Oregon coast make sure you keep an eye out for those sneaker waves!

We are headed to Pacific City next week; I'll send you some pictures later on. Hope you guys are having a great time looking forward to your next email.

Take care, Larie'

Agatha told Frank it was hard to believe that a wave could come up that fast and wipe out someone. She had heard of sneaker waves before but this is the first time that she ever heard of it happening to somebody that she knew. She told Frank she was glad that they didn't run into any skunks while they were in Oregon. It's bad enough having to watch out for snakes. Aggie told Frank how much she enjoyed Larie' letters, they sure are having an interesting time. There always something going on with them.

They had heard about a ranch not too far away that was adopting mules that they had rescued from the Grand Canyon. They decided to drive over and check them out. There was supposed to be a petting zoo there, and if you wanted to adopt one you could. The idea was to inform people of the wild mules in the canyons that had been let go in the years of the gold rush.

When they arrived at the ranch they were surprised to see so many little donkeys/mules. Aggie told Frank that she would have loved to take a couple of them home, but that wasn't goanna happen anytime soon.

As they were wandering around an old miner looking guy, either he was or he was a great actor. He came up to them and said, "Howdy, I'm Mike the owner. Agatha and Frank replied back "Howdy! Mike asked them do you have any questions. Aggie replied "Yes, what is the difference between a Donkey and a Mule? Mike didn't miss a step. He smiled and said I'm glad you asked, "Well, the first difference between a Donkey and a Mule is related to its reproductive system. Donkeys can reproduce but Mules do not reproduce. A Mule is in fact sterile.

Another difference is that there are 62 chromosomes in a Donkey and 63 chromosomes in a Mule."

"Another thing is a Mule has more stamina than a Donkey. The characteristic of the Mule is attributed to its hybrid origin. A Mule also has the capability to jump up a few feet from standing position where as a Donkey cannot perform such an act.

It is said that Mules are more intelligent than Donkeys. Mules have ears smaller than the Donkeys but they are longer and also have almost the same shape of a Horse. A Mule looks like a Donkey with its short thick head, thin limbs, and short mane but it appears different from the Donkey in height, shape of neck, coat and teeth. The Mules are also taller than the Donkeys."

Now you know more than you ever wanted to know about mules and donkeys. Frank smiled and told Mike thanks for the info. Then Frank asked, Mike how many times a day do you get asked that question? Mike just smiled back, pretty much every other person I talk to. Then Mike turned and called back have a nice day and off he went to visit with another customer.

Agatha reminded Frank of the time that they were in Italy and they rented the "four persons bicycle cars" and went for a ride with Beth and Doug. The donkey was standing on the other side of the fence watching them, acting like the Keystone Cops, and you acted like you fell out of the car. We were all laughing, then the donkey joined in with us, and started he haw at you. Frank replied, yea, that donkey sure enjoyed himself.

They continued to wander around the farm. They went into the barn where they discovered this was the place they kept their Colts. "The Colts knew how to work a crowd; they came over to the fence and put their head out so they could be petted. Aggie fell in love with them all. Frank finally pulled her away, and said let's go get something to eat. They stopped at a pub on the way home; they featured fried dill pickles, and alligator nuggets. Aggie ordered a side of both, she loved dill pickles and she always wanted to try alligator, so why not. Surprisingly, they were tasty she got Frank to try a couple of fried pickles. He said not bad, how do you like the Alligator? Not bad, it tastes like chicken, but more chewy then chicken. Frank tried one and really didn't care for it. Aggie enjoyed trying new things, Frank not so much. He use to, but he pretty much eats hamburgers now, if he orders in a pub.

On the road back to the campground, they were following a Class A motorhome; it was a very nice size one too, by the looks of it. He was going at a pretty good speed, so they just followed him. Frank told Aggie, he better slow down, the road up ahead isn't that great. All of sudden they heard this awful sound, and then the Class A started swerving and hit its brakes. In the same instant a big old truck came from the other direction.

The Class A in front of them pulled over, so they did too. They both got out of their Jeep to see if they could help. They weren't sure what had happen, but Aggie figured she should stop. The truck from the other direction just kept on going. He probably didn't even know that the Class A had hit the bridge railing on the right side of the rig.

As Aggie and Frank walked over to the Class A, the couple came out of their RV, they looked pretty shook up. Frank asked them if they were okay and they said yes. The guy from the RV said he wasn't sure what the hell happened. As they walked to the side of the RV they discovered a huge gouge on the side of the rig, going from the middle of the RV to almost the end. He had run the RV along the railing of the bridge. There wasn't much else they could do, and since nobody was injured, they all loaded up and headed to the campground. As they were driving back Frank told Aggie, I don't know how he managed to do that. But I'm sure glad it wasn't us!

After hanging around the area for a few days, Aggie and Frank decided to head up to Fort Sill, and check it out. Frank as usual always wanted to visit Army Posts whenever he was near one. It was because he had retired from the Army. "Once a lifer, all ways a lifer!" The post wasn't that far from where they were at, but they decided to take the RV and maybe camp on the post while they were up there. Once on Post, it wasn't hard to find, to find a parking space where they could leave the RV, while they checked out the post.

It was getting pretty warm in the RV for the dogs though, so they decided they had better find a place to park the RV and set up camp. After running around the post, but after for 30 minutes they couldn't figure out where the Army Travel Campground was located. About the time that they were going to give up they saw a sign that said "Campground" and it pointed in the direction they had not been on yet.

They figured the campground wouldn't be too far away so they went back to where they had parked the RV and drove the direction they had just came from. They drove the RV around from one place to another trying to find the campground. At one point they even found themselves on a road to the live firing range. They followed the sign to the next sign but still no campground, but they still have not found the Army Travel campground. There were only the two signs and nothing else to give them an idea where to go next.

They finally headed out to the other side of the post, and to find another place to camp off post. That's when they saw the Travel Campground; it was in the middle of nowhere. You could tell that it had been flooded earlier in the week, but there were a few spaces that had dried out, that looked like they could park in.

It was a self-service campground; they just had to call a number to let them know they would be staying the night there. When Aggie called the number and talked to the individual, she was told by them that the spaces were all reserved and they couldn't stay there. Needless to say, that didn't make them too happy, but there wasn't much they could do about it.

They continued though a nearby gate and headed down the road to find an off post RV campground. They ended up in Anadarko, OK which was about a 30 minute drive from the post. Again it was a self-service RV campground; they accidentally found this one too. It was at the City Park, with really nice grassy areas. The river was running through the middle of the park, and no one was parked at the campground. There was a sign that said to call the police department, which Aggie did. They told her to come down and pay a $10 fee and they would have a policeman come out and unlock the power box.

After waiting for the police for two hours, Aggie called the police department and asked when they were going to come out and unlock the box. The officer told her, that she figured there was not a big hurry, because she heard them say they were going out for dinner, when they came in to pay their deposit. She told Aggie they would be there in fifteen minutes. Sure enough two police cars pulled up to their RV. Frank and Aggie looked at each other, and Frank said, "How's that for service?" Aggie replied back, I'm just glad we're not doing anything illegal.

Here's a little history on Anadarko, Ok. It is a pretty big town, but it looked pretty empty. "Anadarko was settled on the western plains of Oklahoma. Anadarko has a rich Native American history. It is the self-proclaimed "Indian Capital of the Nation." Native Americans make up the near-majority of the population. The town got its name when its post office was established in 1873. The designation came from the Nadarko Indians, a branch of the Caddo, and the "A" was added by clerical error. In 1871, the Wichita Agency was reestablished on the north bank of the Washita River after being destroyed in the American Civil War. The Wichita Agency administered the affairs of the Wichita, Caddo and other tribes. In 1878, the Kiowa-Comanche Agency at Fort Sill was consolidated with the Wichita Agency".

"In 1901, the federal government allotted the lands of the Kiowa, Comanche and Arapaho Reservations, and opened the surplus land to white settlement. On August 6, 1901, an auction was held for homesteads and town lots. Around 5,000 people were living in "Rag Town" on the east edge of Anadarko awaiting the auction. Anadarko is named after the Nadaco, a Caddo band now affiliated with the Caddo Nation. In the Caddo language, *Nadá-kuh*, means "bumblebee place". The Caddo are a federally recognized American Indian tribe for which Caddo County is named; Caddo County is part of the former reservation of the Caddo, Wichita."

The next day, they met a couple of ladies from the Chamber of Commerce that were out for a walk in the park. They wanted to know how Aggie and Frank liked their campground. Aggie told them it's great and it has nice walking paths. Aggie asked the ladies about their town. She told them that it looked like it was quite the town in its hay day, what happened to it? Thelma told them that before World War II, the soldiers would come up from Fort Sill on buses. They would spend their weekends enjoying the city. At one time the Fort told them they needed to get the prostitutes under control. The soldiers were getting diseases from them. Aggie had to laugh, and told Frank some things just don't change do they! Frank just glared at her and then smiled!

Then when World War II happened, all the soldiers went away. The town just kind of died and never came back. The soldier's families moved away as time went on until it was left empty. Frank told them, he had noticed that a lot of the cars had unusual license plates. They had the tribe they were from on it, he guessed. She told him, you're right, and their very proud of their tribes. She continued to tell them about the town and the people in it. After awhile Thelma and her friend said their goodbyes. They thanked them for staying at their campground. The next morning they headed to Kansas, they were hoping to make it to Dodge City.

After an uneventful trip across the prairies, they made it to the outside of Dodge City around

6pm. They found a campground there that was set up like a little western town with an old west as their landscaping, and it was called Gunsmoke RV Park. It was nice and clean and it was far enough away from town that you didn't have to hear the traffic and city noises. It didn't take long to get set up. They were only going to spend two nights, and their plan was to check out Dodge City and then head toward Utah.

Aggie wanted to go visit her family for a few weeks, and check out the National Parks in Utah. Her family use to go visit the parks when she was young. But it's been a long time since she had seen them. Frank hasn't really seen Utah. The only thing he has seen is from the freeway.

Aggie was checking her gmail and saw she had gotten an email from Larie'. She told Frank she had received the letter. He told her to read it out loud to him. She told him they haven't left Oregon yet.

Hi Aggie,

It sounds like you guys are having a good time. I'm glad you were able to visit Frank's old friend in Holly Beach, Louisiana. The pictures you sent are really cool I've never seen houses on stilts like that before. Yea it was a little scary having the sneaker wave trying to drag us back into the ocean but we survived. We spent the last couple weeks in Pacific city at Thousand Trails. It was an

51

interesting two weeks. When we first got there they told us there was no water on the lower part of the property, they said it would only be a couple days so we decided to park where we could have septic. We did have water in our water tank so it was no big deal at that point.

Well a week and half later we still didn't have water. Something about they had to order a 4 inch pipe from the East Coast before they could repair the pipe. But that was okay it was kind of fun, we filled up gallon jugs every time we went in and out of the property and put it in our water tank no big deal. Then they had a power outage, from our understanding lightning hit a transformer by a school. When they went to repair it they blew out the other transformers that were connected to it. We decided to go out for dinner, but discovered that the power was out for about 30 miles away. So we ended up going to Lincoln city to have dinner.

On the way home we noticed that all the power was on in the different buildings. So we figured we would have power when we got back to the RV, but no luck. We ended up not getting the power until about 11 o'clock that night. To top it all off our satellite wouldn't work where we were located at, we didn't even have antenna service, Wi-Fi or cell phone service. All in all it was pretty much a dead zone for us. It is a really nice campground, if you're not a full time traveler. We were there last summer and it was pretty full with all of the summer vacationers. They all looked like they were having a great time!

As usual the weather was rainy and windy, but we did drive on to the beach and park. The waves were pretty big, so we kept an eye on them. The dogs enjoy running on the beach, after awhile the water was getting a little too close for us. Besides it is the only place we can connect to WIFI here. I remember you telling me about the car that got stuck in the sand at Cape Kiwanda; we didn't want to take any chances.

Well were headed to Whaler Cove again, it's one of our favorite places to go on the Oregon Coast. I hope this letter fines you in good health. Dean has been doing great, he is up to two miles a day, and we hope to get to five, in the next couple of months. He is in pain a lot, but he tries not to complain about it. I keep telling him he needs to tell me, so when we go to the doctor I can tell them how he really feels. You know guys when their doctor asks them how their doing they say, "I'm doing well!" I'm just happy he is doing so great.

Tell Frank Hi! Hope everything is going great for you guys, looking forward to hearing from you. Keep sending pictures!

Larie'

Frank reminded Aggie that they had been there and Larie' was right about it being a dead zone. Aggie replied back yea, but it is a beautiful area. I loved the beach there and all the cool things to see. Frank replied, yea, driving on the beach is the best part. It's great to hear Dean is doing so well. I really didn't think he would be walking that far already. I guess he is a fighter; he told me there was no way he was going back to a wheelchair, if there is anything he can do about it.

The next morning they headed into Dodge City, it looked like a modern day Western town. It had the saloons, tourist attractions and stores to buy keepsakes. They drove to the other end of town where the stockyards and train station was for loading up the cattle. It didn't smell too good so they headed back to camp. They had been there years ago before it became a modern day Western exhibit. Aggie told Frank her favorite place to visit the Old West is still Gammon Gulch in AZ. She would rather see real artifacts and authentic old west things than to buy things in a store for keepsakes. Frank agreed with her, but the towns do have to make a living. When they got back to the RV they did the normal route of taking the dogs out for a walk and checking out the campground.

The dog walk was on top of the hill, they were surprised that the view was so incredible. There were open fields and horses wandering around the fields. About that time they got a call from Aggies's mother.

After a few minutes her mother asked her, "How much longer will it be before they would be there?" Aggie told her it should be about a week or two; they wanted to check out a couple National Parks on their way there. Why is there a problem, she asked her Mom. Her Mom said no she just was anxious to see her. The family was looking forward to seeing her and Frank again.

Then her mom told her not to stop and check out any parks in Utah on their way there. It was supposed to be a surprise, but her Mom couldn't keep the secret. She told Aggie, we bought a trailer, it's 30 feet long with two doors and we want to go travel around Utah with you guys. It sounds like you kids are having so much fun. We can't leave the place for very long, but figure we could travel around Utah with you.

Aggie looked at Frank; he just smiled and said Great! Aggie told her mom that would be awesome looking forward to traveling with you guys. They talked for a little while longer and then Aggie told her we will talk to you soon, love you and hung up the phone. It was time to get back to the RV, it was starting to get dark and the dogs were bored waiting for Aggie to get off the phone.

Frank asked Aggie, so what do you think of the idea of traveling around with your parents. I think it's wonderful; I would love to see them out and about. What do you think, Frank? Great, it'll be fun to have them around. They are always up for new things.

They headed back to the RV to have dinner and get settled in for the night. Frank opened up the U.S. map to see which road they should take out of Dodge City. They were planning on hanging out in Kansas for another week, but he guessed that plan would be cancelled. He showed Aggie the map and suggested that they take Hwy 70, and they could stop in Colorado Springs and check out Ft. Carson. Aggie smiled and kissed him and said sounds like a plan. After being married for 40 years, they really didn't have to say much to each other. He knew Aggie was missing her family, and was ready to go home, and Aggie knew if there was an Army post around they would have to stop. They had been stationed at Ft. Carson many years ago. It would be fun to check out the old neighborhood.

They wanted to leave early to beat the heat, it was suppose to be in the 80s by the afternoon tomorrow. The air conditioner in the driver area of the RV doesn't work so it gets pretty hot in the cab by midday. Even with the windows open, it doesn't help too much. As they head west the temperature will be much nicer to travel in during the day. Aggie was glad the air condition works great in the Jeep.

CHAPTER 6

Colorado adventures

They figure it's going to take about eight hours to get to Ft. Carson. They had lived in Colorado Springs for two years. Ft. Carson was at the foot of the Cheyenne Mt., outside of Colorado Springs. They had the two girls, Twila and Maria there, Frank was two at the time. They purchased a nice little three bedroom house, with a basement and a large yard. Then Frank got levied to Korea for a one year tour, so they sold the house and Aggie moved home to Utah to be with her family. With their three kids and she needed to get a job to help support the family. Frank was only a Spec. 5 at that point. The money was tight with one household, but with two households Frank will need money to live on. Aggie still needed to pay bills and feed the kids. The good part was they cleaned 5k for their house, so they could pay off a lot of their bills.

That night they stopped in Lamar, CO, it was a small town; the campground was a Mom and Pop place. It had a building with a shower on one end and a little café on the other end. It was a cute little café with pictures of the area. They arrived just in time for dinner, it was great food. As usual Frank had a hamburger and Aggie had a steak dinner, with baked potatoes. Aggie loves her steak!

According to the flyer on the table, the town is located along Route 50 and home to one of the Colorado's welcome centers. Lamar is a small place to start a journey to the state. The staff at the welcome center will not only detail the history of Lamar, but will also give visitors brochures and maps covering the whole state."

"The welcome center is also a bit of an attraction itself. It is located in a restored 1907 train depot; the center features a train engine and 100-year-old windmill and water tank. It's the only location to include all three elements in a historic depot. Located near the huge cottonwoods that lined the Arkansas River north of town. The Big Timber Museum provides artifacts and information on frontier life, the historic dust bowl days and the site of Camp Apache National historic landmark, and a Japanese-American internment camp. It also hosts a High Plains Snow Goose Festival. Each year that brings in a lot of the tourists to Lamar's beautiful plains setting. There are other attractions including the Madonna of the trail Monument, an 18 foot high tribute to the women of the covered wagon days.

They had walked the girls before heading over to eat, so when they got back, they let the girls out and they sat out and watched the sunset. The colors were beautiful, orange, pink, blue and yellow. They could hear the frogs in the distance; they could see the highway from their place. It was empty. They started a fire and started talking about their life in Colorado Springs.

The next morning they got up early, Aggie decided to check her email to see if there was any interesting to read. She had received another letter from Larie'. It was a short letter this time, Aggie read it to Frank.

Hello from Oregon,

Just wanted to send you a short note to let you know were still alive here in Oregon. We have spent the last three weeks in Newport, the weather is still rainy but we did get a couple good days so we could walk on the beach. The tide is still coming in pretty far and actually is hitting against the banks. Of course, it's been pretty windy here to, up to 65 mile an hour winds. We hope to be leaving the coast in the next couple weeks and heading in land. Dean is doing much better and we would like to get some place where we could walk without getting soaked. The plan is to head to Riddle, Oregon and then go to Ashland, OR and then head east. Dean wants to see his sister in Grand Junction Colorado.

Other than the weather there hasn't been much to talk about. Spring break has come and gone, there were a lot of kids running around here, there must have been 30 kids in the campground. They had lots of activities for them to keep busy. Kinda excited about leaving the coast line, we have always liked Eastern Oregon. Dean spent a few years in Riddle, Oregon when he was a little kid; he wants to go check it out.

It sounds like you guys are having fun traveling, every time I read your letters it gets me antsy, because I want to do the same thing, I want to live the Dream too! Hopefully, in the next few weeks we will be able to head east. After listening to your stories about Austin, Nevada, and your hometown of Delta, Utah, we decided that were going to take Highway 50 through Nevada and Utah to Colorado. Maybe, if it works out we will be able to meet up somewhere. From our understanding you and Frank were planning on visiting your parents in Delta. Let us know when that will be and hopefully we can set up our time to be there to. We would love to go fossil hunting and rock hounding with you. I'll let you know when we get closer.

Take care, Larie'

Frank told Aggie it'll be nice to see them again. Yea, I feel like we have known each other for years. Then Frank added you know I'm looking forward to see Ft. Carson for only being there for two years; we sure had a lot of memories there. Remember the first day, when the moving trucks delivered our furniture. We lived on a road that had a hill, and there was snow and ice on it. The neighbor kids were sledding down it, and one of them lost control and went under the moving truck and hit his head. Aggie had to laugh. Yeah, that should have told us it was going to be an interesting place, I'm glad he didn't get hurt, although he did make quite the loud thud when he hit.

That's all it took to get the memories going. Remember Harold our Australian Shepherd we got as a puppy. He loved to go into the garden and chew on our cucumbers and ran up and down the fence line to play with the dog next-door. He wiped out our corn that we had growing along the fence in the garden. Frank said yeah he was a cutie but a handful. Remember the dog house I built? Agatha said yes it must've weighed 300 pounds as much wood and nails you put into it. Yea, but it was nice and warm and kept the rain out, Frank replied to her.

How about the time that you brought home the 14 foot heat duct? That you found on the side of the road. You brought it home in our little VW Rabbit, and it was sticking out about 6 feet out of the back of the Rabbit hatch. She said yes, the funny part was watching Janice holding on to it. She was lying down in the passenger seat holding onto to it so it wouldn't fall out of the car. Oh and don't forget the railroad tie that I brought home. I was always finding something that we could use at the house.

Aggie asked Frank, remember when I got 3$^{rd\circ}$ degree burns on my legs from being out in the sun when we were out at the lake. I was 7 months pregnant I couldn't walk because of the burns on my legs, so you had to carry me everywhere. Then one day when you went back to work Frank Jr. figured out that I couldn't chase him so he took off out the door and ran out into the field next to our trailer house. I had to chase him down. I just had enough energy to call you and tell you to come home (NOW).

Man you scared the hell out of me, at first I thought you were in labor. Aggie laughed and said I wish it would have been less painful. I felt like I had a thousand needles going into my legs. Frank Jr. just looked at me like I was crazy. I was so glad we had that play pen for me to put him in; there was no way I could have run after him again.

Frank reminded Aggie about the time Frank Jr. turned the garden hose on her, so you couldn't come out the front door. You had to go out the back door and sneak around the trailer to get him, while I kept his attention.

Aggie pointed down at her legs, I still have the discolored skin from it. Frank responded back with, "The doctor sure did give you hell for not coming in sooner." Yeah well, lesson learned I guess, don't sit out in the sun with white legs, when you're on top of a mountain, Aggie said as she smiled at him. The expression on your face when you came into the trailer was pretty funny too, she told Frank. Frank replied you scared the hell out of me.

The evening was filled with memories, they both enjoyed living in their little blue house on Shaw Ave. It was just the beginning of their life together. Their family was complete, they only wanted three children. They had a wonderful house, and they both loved their jobs. Frank was in the Army and Aggie raising their three little ones and going to college to get her degree in teaching. It is hard to believe how far they have come.

They left Lamar, CO in the early morning and were more excited than ever to see their old house and neighborhood. Five hours later they arrived in Colorado Springs. This time Aggie went on line and found where the Post Travel Campground was, they didn't want to repeat the Ft. Sill nightmare. It was on the out skirts of the post. But they decided against going there and went to a newer campground; it looked pretty nice on the web site. It had trees and looked pretty clean. It had a fence around it with security guards. They always felt better when there was security around. They always had a car full of items they put in a tent, when there wasn't any security. But this time they could put everything underneath the RV and not really worry about anyone taking it.

They were only going to stay for a couple of days and check out the old neighborhood. They were setting up camp when a middle-aged couple stopped by to say hi, they introduced themselves as Tom and Sue and asked Frank how long they were planning on staying. Frank told them, and then they continued to talk about the area. Aggie didn't like the way they were looking around the outside of the RV, and the girls didn't seem too friendly towards them either. They talked to them for a little bit longer, and then Frank told them they needed to get going. They wanted to go into town and see their old house and have some dinner. They said their goodbyes and Tom and Sue walked away. Aggie turned to Frank and asked if they seemed strange to him? Frank replied back, I think I'll make sure to put all the little stuff inside the RV, and lock up the RV before we go. Aggie nodded her head and agreed with him. They loaded up the dogs and headed out the security gate, the security guard waved at him to stop and told them they had a new code to get into the gate. Frank thanked them and asked, "Where is a good place to eat around here? Joe, the security guard, told them there is a nice little diner down the road. Frank said thanks we will give it a try and drove down the road.

When they arrived in the old neighborhood they spotted their house, it was now white instead of baby blue. The tree that saved Frank Jr. and Twila's life by stopping the truck was huge now. As soon as they saw it, Frank told Aggie, if only that tree could talk. It would say remember that night when the neighbors truck from up the street, came rolling down the hill and was headed toward the kid's bedroom, and I (the tree) stood up to it and stopped it right in its tracks. If it wasn't for me, who knows what could have happened to them. I may have been small at that time, but I was big enough to stop that old truck with my trunk. Aggie turned to Frank and laughed, I didn't know you talked tree. But you're right it did save our kid's lives.

Aggie told Frank, I'm sure that's what the tree would have said, as she smiled and laughed. I'm so glad they didn't cut it down. Frank replied, "Me too, and gave her a hug. They decided they better go eat. They decided to go to a little diner that Joe suggested; it was close to the campground.

As they were waiting for the waitress to come take their order, Frank got a call on his cell phone. He answered and got this weird look on his face. What? What? Are the dogs all right? Okay! Oh, good! But! But! Okay! We are on the way. Aggie was getting scared but she followed Frank out to their car. As they headed towards the camp, Aggie said "Tell me, tell me what's wrong." Frank told her he didn't know for sure, something about someone tried to steal our RV. He said they had everything under control, but we need to come back to the camp. He said he would explain everything when we got back to the campground. Then he just hung up like he was in a hurry.

All the way back they could not think of what could possibly be wrong. As they pulled up to the gate, they couldn't believe their eyes. There were a couple of police cars and police officers walking around their RV. There stood Sue and Tom in handcuffs! Their Penelope parked just inside of the gate, and no sign of the dogs.

Frank and Aggie were speechless. Joe the security guard walked over to them and told them to leave their car outside the gate for now. Then he said "Come with me!" They followed him over to the small guard station, where the police were standing. She could hear their dogs barking inside of their RV. Aggie didn't wait for permission; she just ran over to the RV and climbed in. She didn't care what the police had to say, she was worried about her girls.

There was an officer inside, at first he told her to stop. Then he looked at Aggie and nodded his head towards the bedroom. He could tell he shouldn't stand in her way. She was on a mission to save her dogs. Aggie hurried into the bedroom, with tears in her eyes. She gathered their dogs up in her arms. They were so happy to see her! They were both on her shoulders, licking away at her face. Frank poked his head in and asked, "Are they okay?" She just smiled and nodded her head yes.

As Frank turned around the County Sheriff said, "Let's all go into the front of the RV, so we can have a talk." Two other deputies and Joe were already sitting on the couch waiting for them to come back in. Aggie handed Frank Susie and she carried Sheba to the front room. There was no way that she was going to leave the dogs behind.

The Sheriff started to talk, "Let me start from the beginning. We have been after these two for some time. We had information that they had stolen a camper and was headed east. We had a license number of the camper that they had stolen earlier, so we alerted all the campgrounds in the area. It took awhile, but we finally heard from Joe. We talked to Joe and he told us that there was a camper in the park with that license number.

We told Joe to shut down the campground, don't let anybody out. The Officer said, Joe told us, he remembers letting you guys out earlier, but you guys didn't match the description of the people we were looking for. You told Joe you were going into town for dinner. Then about 30 minutes later your RV started coming towards the gate. This set off a red light in Joe's head.

When they pulled up to the gate Joe informed them that there was an issue with the gate, so he couldn't let anyone out right now. Joe spoke up, "Yeah that's right, I thought it was strange, with you guys leaving earlier in your car and not telling me that someone else was taking your RV. It just didn't feel right, and once I saw who they were I asked them for their ID. They were smiling at me and the man said they were friends of yours. They said Frank had asked them to pick up the RV for him and take it to have some maintenance done on it.

That's when Joe started to get excited, "Then it hit me, they were the ones the cops were looking for! I pulled out my gun and told them to get out of the RV. Just then the police car pulled up to the gate, they saw that I had my gun pulled out. It was a good thing I knew them, as he looked at the sheriff and smiled.

Thank you Joe that was very brave of you, said Agatha. "Well I have to tell you I was quite shaken up about all this. It was the first time I've had to pull my gun on anyone," Joe told her.

Frank and Aggie were sitting there holding onto their precious little dogs, trying to calm them down. They were wide-eyed and taking it all in. There was no way they were going to leave Frank and Aggies's laps.

The sheriff continued, "My officers have been trying to find some witnesses, but no one heard or saw anything. As you can see they busted open the door and hotwired your RV. They must have been getting pretty desperate to try to steal your rig.

Now Frank, can you tell me anything? The sheriff asked. Frank and Aggie both told them about meeting the couple earlier that day.

Frank said they had just gotten their RV unloaded; they were only planning on staying for a few days. They were relaxing outside when a couple came strolling by. They stopped and said hi and admired our little dogs. We didn't think much about it, it happens all the time in campgrounds.

They introduced themselves as Sue and Tom Jones. They really like our RV and asked a lot of questions about it. They mention they had a camper and were thinking about getting something a little bit bigger. Frank smiled and said I had no idea they were talking about our rig.

The Joneses seem to be very nice couple in the beginning, Frank told the sheriff, I could tell Aggie really wasn't sure about them; I could tell by the way she was acting. Normally, she offers them a drink and asks them to sit down, but this time she just stood there looking at them.

The Officer asked them, can you give us a description of them for our report. Frank told him, "Sue was a small blonde woman; she was wearing jeans and simple green shirt. Tom was a rather stocky bald man, not much taller than his wife. I'm assuming that is who you have in the police car! Frank pointed to their cop car. Frank continues, she asked if it was hard taking pets along when they traveled. Aggie being very proud of her little girls, she told them, they are very well behaved. Frank spoke up and said, "We can leave them in the RV if we want to go out to dinner. They just make themselves comfortable in the bedroom." Aggie noted Sue gave Tom a kind of knowing look. Maybe they were thinking about getting a pet. I think they planned on stealing our dogs too, as her face started to get red. She mumbles under her breath for a few seconds, and waited for Frank to continue.

Frank said the girls were not very friendly towards the couple either. Normally, they would be all over their company. Something didn't feel right so I looked at Aggie and told her if we were going out to eat we better get going. That's when I told Sue and Tom, "If you will excuse us, we need to really get going, it was nice to meet you." Tom replied, "Nice talking to you, see you!" Sue and Tom left and we locked the RV and drove off. Aggie added to the sheriff, I thought for a minute Frank was going to invite them along. Frank had told me, I didn't know why I felt they were over friendly, now we know why. For some reason they made me feel uneasy.

When they finished their statement, the Sheriff said he would get in touch with them if they needed anything else. But if you could stay another day that would be great, just in case we need something else. Frank and Aggie agreed to stay until they didn't need them anymore, besides they were going to have to fix the door and the ignition before they could go anywhere.

As everyone was leaving Joe told Frank that the park would take care of fixing the damage to the RV. Later that evening Aggie said, "I can't believe this happened to us." Well so much for leaving early tomorrow. Frank reminds Aggie we haven't eaten yet! Aggie replied back, well I'm not going anywhere tonight; I'll just cook something here. Anything special you want? Oh sweetie anything is fine, Frank told her. Aggie smiled and said, good Tuna Helper it is!

The next morning Joe came by and said the sheriff had called and said they could go ahead and leave. They had their information and if they need anything they would give them a call. He also told them there was no charge for the next couple days if they wanted to stay. The repair guys will be out later today to fix everything. Aggie turned to Frank and said let's leave tomorrow; my families are waiting for us.

They loaded everything up that afternoon and figured they would head out mid morning; they should only have to stay out two more days. Then they should be in Utah.

The repairman fixed everything that afternoon, and they changed their minds and planed on leaving early the next morning. They wanted to reach Grand Junction, CO, and see a few old friends.

Everything went off as planned; they were on the road by 7 a.m. After being on the road for a couple of hours, Frank remarked earlier what a nice day it was and there was not much traffic so it should be easy sailing.

Then Frank called Aggie on the walkie talkie. Aggie you're not going to believe what I'm seeing. Aggie replied what is it? "It's some old guy in the middle of the highway, in the medium. Cars aren't slowing down; they're just honking at him. I'm going to stop and see if we can help him." As Frank pulled over the RV and Aggie pulled up right behind him, the man started to move toward them. Aggie got out of the car and walked towards the RV. She could see the man jumping up and down waving at them.

As Aggie got closer to the RV Frank came out of it with a blanket in hand. Aggie said are you sure you want to do this? Hell yes the guys in trouble, why else would he be out here doing that. If not I think I can take him, he told her. Aggie stayed by their RV just in case, something went wrong. Frank waited for the traffic to clear then he went over to where the guy was. Hey buddy what's the problem? Frank asked him. The guy replied thank goodness, "Please help me!" The guy said. "Nobody would stop for me; I don't know where I am. Frank asked, is that why you took your clothes off, to get some attention? The guy looked down and saw he was naked, he looked even more upset. He was so confused.

Before Frank left Aggie he had told her to call 911. Frank told the poor guy don't worry we'll help you out, as Frank handed him the blanket. He reached out for it and took the blanket, and covered himself up. Where are your clothes Frank asked, the guys replied, I don't know where they are.

Aggie walked over to them and she could see he was an elderly man, disoriented, and at this point very cold. He told Frank "I don't know how I got here; I'm not even sure what my name is." Frank told him let's go to our RV so you can get warmed up and wait for the police to arrive. As they were walking over to the RV he discovered the man's clothes on the ground and Frank picked them up, and handed them to Aggie to carry back to the RV. Aggie looked for some kind of ID, but there wasn't any ID, no wallet or anything. As they got over to the RV help arrived, it was the police and an ambulance.

The police officer walked up to Frank and the gentleman and said we have been looking everywhere for him. The officer asked Frank if he knew him. Frank replied no sir; we just stopped to help the poor guy. "Well thanks Mr., we'll take care of him from here." They had put him into the ambulance, and the medic was closing the doors to ambulance, when the guy pokes his head out and said, "Thank you for your kindness!" Frank waved at him and said no problem.

As they walked back to their RV Frank said, that was quick, it didn't take them long to get here. Aggie asked Frank, what was his name? Beats me, he didn't know and the police didn't tell me. Well that was quite an experience. I'm just grateful that we were able to help.

They loaded up and headed west toward Durango, CO. They were hoping that the rest of the trip was uneventful. But no such luck! It was a dry sunny day; the goal was to get across the Continental divide before the storm front came in. The prediction for the weekend was 1 to 2 feet of snow in the mountain passes.

Aggie was enjoying the landscape; each valley they drove into had a different view. She thought to herself, this is why we love to travel. Each state has a variation of landscapes and rock formations. They were driving along the back road, that's where you see the real country side.

Everything was running smoothly, they had just driven out of Gunnison and had gone about 15 miles when all of a sudden, she heard an explosion. It was their RV tire; the outside rear dual had exploded. Aggie was surprised she heard the explosion from inside the Jeep.

The next thing she knew there was rubber flying up at her. She swerved to avoid the pieces. First there were small pieces coming from the back of the RV. All of a sudden, a large chunk of rubber flew from underneath the RV. It rolled into the other lane; it happen so fast she didn't even have time to swerve, it just flew passed her. Lucky there was no oncoming traffic.

She radioed Frank of the situation and of course he all ready knew that something bad had happened. He didn't reply right away, he was trying to stop the

RV and pulled it off the road. Then she heard Frank say Son of...., what was that!

There wasn't much room for him to pull off the RV, as far as Aggie could see. As Aggie pulled up behind him and got out of the Jeep and headed to the RV, Frank came out the door. They both walked over to the tire that blew. Sure enough the outside dual had blown off the outer casing. Passing cars were cutting it pretty close to their rig. There was no way that they would be able to change the tire where they were at.

Aggie asked Frank, did you hear the explosion? He replied, yes I heard the bang from the rear of the coach, and then there was a noticeable thumbing sound. Then it felt like driving over rumble strips, like the ones they put along the edge of the driving lane. He said he knew at once it had to be a blowout. I was driving about 63 miles an hour, so it took several hundred feet to come to stop. Luckily there was a wide shoulder to pull off onto just a little ways down the road.

The first thing Frank noticed was the driver side outside dual obviously had blown. The casing was misshaped and looked wrinkled. There was a trace of smoke still coming off of it, and it looked smaller than normal. No doubt because the entire outer tread had been blown off and it had only the inner casing and still belt exposed where the tread should have been. The weight of the entire RV was now being carried by the single inner duel. He looked down the road and saw where it had landed, in the middle of the road about 50 yards away.

The next thing they noticed was something dripping from the storage compartment area, which was located behind the blown tire. Frank thought to himself that could not be a good thing since the compartment contained the plumbing for the black and gray water evacuation ports (sewage dump area). When he opened the compartment hatch cover to check the damage, he saw that the outer wall had taken the direct hit from the flopping tire tread and had been totally crushed. The storage area behind the tire was crushed and had a big hole in it. All the contents in it, the tools, sewer hoses, and all the other things had been jumbled up. The sewer line coming from the black water tank was the problem. Fortunately, they had emptied the tank before leaving the last campground. But it still had water in it and it was steadily dripping onto the road.

Frank started pulling stuff out of the compartment; Aggie went and got the laundry basket so he had something to put it in. Frank started loading it up with all the items that were in the compartment. Then they could see the gaping hole better. The box had been welded to the inner body of the coach, it wasn't anymore. After they unloaded everything into the laundry basket they carried it around to the other side, to get out of the way of the traffic. It wasn't slowing down for them.

They couldn't believe how bad the tire was. Aggie figured she would just call for assistance and have someone come out and put the spare on. Without the right tools, it would be impossible for them to change it.

When she looked at her phone, she discovered that there was no cell service. She thought great when you need the phone there is no service! Then she looked down the road, the traffic was going around the big chunk of rubber lying in the middle of the road, it had landed by the line, so they had to swerve to the right to avoid hitting it and they were getting awful close to their rig. She told Frank, we need to get off this road.

Then she suggested to Frank that she would go ahead in the Jeep and see if there was someplace that they could pull into so they could get off of the road. He agreed she had driven about three miles when she found a gravel pit, but there was a red truck blocking part of the driveway. It also had a flat! The driver was gone; she wasn't sure if Frank could get the RV passed it to get into the gravel pit.

There was still no cell service, anywhere in the valley. Aggie drove up the road a little farther and couldn't find any place that they could pull off the road. She turned around and went back to where Frank was she saw another RV parked behind the rig.

But before she stopped, she wanted to remove the big chunk of rubber that was still in the middle of the road. She drove past them and went down the road, and pulled off to the side and got out to remove the big hunk of rubber; she put it on the side of the road. Then she turned the Jeep around again and pulled in front of their RV. She got out of the Jeep and went over to Frank and the stranger to see what was going on. Frank introduced Larry; he was older gentleman and a very, very tan guy. He had told Frank that he had everything they would need to change the tire, an electric impact wrench, jacks, etc. He said it was a good thing that they had duals on the back and it was the outside tire. They could drive on the good tire still, Frank didn't look to sure about it, but they had no choice.

They all loaded up and headed towards the gravel pit. Larry put his walkie talkie on the same channel as theirs, so he could hear what was going on with them. Aggie drove ahead of them, as she drove up to the red truck; she had noticed that there was enough room to pull the RV's in. By swinging wide, they could go behind the red truck, to get into the gravel pit. As they pulled into the gravel pit, they could see there was plenty of room for both of the RVs to park and work on changing the tire.

Larry was a full-time traveler, and he called himself an Escapee. He had been at it for a while so he had everything they could possibly need to put a spare tire on. Neither one of them had a big enough jack that would go high enough to remove the flat. Larry came up with the idea of driving the good tire on top of a couple of 2" boards, it would raise it about

4 inches then they could put the jacks on top of the other boards they had to jack it up even higher. It worked!

It was quite the show Aggie just stood there freezing to death; the wind was blowing pretty hard. Aggie moved the Jeep so it would block the wind from the guys, as they worked on removing the tire. Frank said that it helped a little. They were hoping that the wind wouldn't blow too hard while they had RV up on jacks.

Then a state trooper showed up, Aggie walked over and explained what was going on. The state trooper asked Aggie, if they knew what happened to the guy that owned the red truck, which was blocking the driveway. Aggie had noticed a guy walking down the road across the road. She told the Trooper she wasn't sure but it looked like it might be the guy walking from that house over there, she pointed in the direction of the gentleman walking down the road. The state trooper thanked her and waited for the gentleman to come to his truck.

Then the next thing you know a CDOT (Colorado Dept. of Transportation) truck pulled into the gravel pit. They looked like they were going to tell them that they can't camp there. Aggie walked over to them and explained what was going on. After she explains to them, they were okay with them being there. Then they went over and talked to the state trooper for a little bit.

Frank and Larry were having problems removing the old tire, but finally got it off. Aggie went over and asked the two younger road crew guys to help install the spare; they agreed and said no problem. It was quite the show, Frank, Larry and the State Trooper all stood there watching the CDOT guys.

They ended up having to dig a 6 inch hole and jacking up the RV from the backside to finally get the new tire to fit into the tire well. After two hours, they finally had the tire replaced. Frank and Aggie thanked them for all their help. Aggie couldn't help it, she had to give Larry a big hug and a thanked him because they couldn't have done it without him. If it wasn't for all of his equipment, there was no way that they could have changed the tire there.

It had gotten late so they decided to turn around and go back 15 miles to the town they had just gone through to spend the night there. Aggie remember seeing a RV campground on the way into town, it looked pretty empty.

The first campground they went to was closed for the winter; they finally found another 3 miles on the other side of town. So they ended up back tracking a total of 18 miles. But they were happy just to find a place to spend the night. It was a nice little campground; the owner had told them there was a storm front coming in tonight. They are expecting snow, maybe a couple of inches tonight. All Aggie and Frank could say was, "Great, that's all we need!" Aggie had told him the story about the blowout and he told them there were a couple of tire shops in town.

Frank couldn't stand it so he had to go work on the sewer line while there is still light out; luckily it had just popped the connection, so he was able to repair it. Aggie was so proud of him; the man can fix anything she thought to herself, the idea of not having a toilet in their RV would have sucked!

The next morning they woke up and sure enough there was snow on the ground, about an inch of it. No big deal as far as Frank and Aggie were concerned. Agatha called the tire shop in town, to see if they had their size tire in stock so they could get a replacement. They really didn't feel comfortable using the spare on the road for any length of time. The spare tire was about 20 years old, but never had been used.

The first shop she called didn't have the space until later that day. The second tire shop said, they had one in stock, and could do it anytime. Aggie told him they would be there within the hour. They told her that would be fine so it was all set up for them to go ahead and get a new tire. Once they arrived it didn't take long for them to remove the old one and put on the new one. He put the spare back under the RV. All Aggie could think was she sure wished they had that fancy floor jack when they were out on the road yesterday.

They loaded up and headed to Durango, it was around 11 o'clock when they finally were able to leave town. They arrived late in Durango, but at least they didn't have any trouble getting there. They had made reservations at the RV campground, so there wasn't any problem getting a space. They did just the basics electricity, water and moved things out of the way inside the RV, so they could go to bed. They planned on leaving first thing in the morning. It didn't take long for them to fall asleep.

They slept in the next morning; it had been a rough couple of days. It didn't take long to get back on the road. They just moved a few boxes, plants and they were on the roads. They were making pretty good time on the back roads. When all of a sudden the chrome wheel cover flew off of the left tire, the one they just had installed. Aggie radioed Frank and told him the hubcap fell off, and to stop the RV! Aggie pulled off the road; she wanted to pick up the hubcap, there was no way she was leaving it behind. Those things are expensive! Good thing she was behind him, she thought to herself, otherwise they would be out a hubcap.

Frank radioed back and asked her what did you say? What is going on? She repeated to him that the hubcap had flown off and she was looking for it. In the meantime Frank couldn't find any place to pull off the RV, so he just stopped on the road. It was a good thing that there was no traffic on the back roads and it was a straight away that he stopped on.

Aggie was surprised she didn't find the hubcap right away. She had to walk up and down the road.

She looked in the creek, hoping it wasn't there, but she couldn't find it anywhere. She walked up and down the area where she saw it come off, but couldn't find it. Then she decided to walk farther up the road, and that's where she found it. Somehow or another it had rolled down the road about 15 feet, and off to the left side of the road, and it was turned upside down in the tall grass. She guessed it wanted to play hide and seek with her. But she did finally find it, she called Frank on the walkie talkie and told him, Okay, were ready to go. Frank radioed back, and said Okay see you in a bit.

Frank found a pull off about twenty miles down the road. It was time to take a break anyway. Frank walked back to the Jeep to check out the wheel cover. After looking at it, he told Aggie, it looks like the tire guy didn't tighten down the nuts; they are still connected to the hub cab. Aggie told him, great at least we don't have to buy anything. Let's go have lunch. Frank replied, good idea, I'm hungry!

After an hour break they got back on the road again. They were going down the road, when Frank radioed Aggie and asked her, why didn't you tell me I had my blinker on? She replied back, because it's not on. Then she heard him ask, is the left one on, she told him no. Damn the blinkers aren't working. Man we got to get out of Colorado, nothing but bad things have been happening to us. Aggie had to agree with him. We only have one more day, and we'll be in Utah.

Around three o'clock they found a RV campground just off the highway, it was a nice little place. It looked like four fifth-wheel trailers were parked there, and there were about twenty more spaces still open. It was another serve yourself place. There was a building in the middle of the campground, which had restroom, shower, and a washer and dryer in it. It had a fence around the whole area. Good thing too, there were cattle on the other side. The girls saw them and they just watched them closely, and growled once in a while. Just to let the cattle know they were in charge, Aggie guessed. They settled in for the night. They had seen a lot of beautiful country side today, and they missed the storm that was coming in. Except for the highway traffic it was a nice little place to stay.

The next morning Frank told Aggie let's make sure we get out of Colorado today and she agreed with him. Hopefully nothing will go wrong for the rest of the trip, while were here in Colorado. Everything was going well as they cruised down the freeway; Aggie had just seen a sign saying 20 miles to the Utah border. She radioed Frank and said almost out of here! When all of a sudden "BANG". Frank looked into his mirror as soon as he heard the bang and he saw a grey cloud of smoke and black chunks flying about. He knew what it was, another blowout. He couldn't believe it, another blowout! This time it was on the passenger side rear.

Aggie was right behind Frank, when she heard the explosion, and the next thing she knew a big chunk of rubber was flying out from underneath the rig. Frank had already started pulling off of the road when she radioed him, I can't believe this shit, another blowout.

Aggie pulled up behind Frank again, talk about déjà vu, but this time it had just happened the day before. In fact the tire looked like the one from yesterday. Frank walked up to Aggie, and said, "What the hell is going on? Aggie couldn't help it she just smiled and said Colorado road gremlins! The good news is this time there was an exit just a little ways up the road so they agreed to go ahead and drive the RV up to the exit.

Aggie spotted an auto shop just down the road, so she drove down there, while Frank parked the RV on level spot. But the place was closed and there was no one around. Aggie drove back up to the RV and checked the phone to see if they had cell service. They did have cell service so she was able to call for help. She called the towing company to have them come out and change the tire, but the guy on the phone told her, it would cost her $200 to have them come out and do it. Before even thinking, Aggie responded you got to be kidding! The guy said, that's what it costs, and then he asked her where you located at? Aggie told him we're at mile marker 26. He told her they are only 5 miles away from them. Why don't you just drive the RV to our location?

That way it won't cost that much to have us replace the tire. Aggie told Frank what he had told her and Frank agreed with them that would be a better plan. They got back in the rigs and headed down the freeway at 35 miles an hour. Now in Colorado the speed limit on the freeway is 70 miles, it's a good thing that our Jeep blinkers were working. It was the longest 5 miles they have driven in a long time.

Just as they were coming up to the first exit, the guy from the tire shop just happened to call and asked where they were. Aggie had told him, we're at the rest area exit. He said turn there, that's our exit. We are to the right. Aggie radioed Frank and told him turn, turn now! Frank almost missed the turn but he did make it. They drove up the exit ramp, looking for the tire shop the guy on the phone said look to the right. Aggie told Frank look to the right and as she said that Frank radio back I see it. Aggie said goodbye to the guy and said I'll see you in a minute.

This was a lot less stressful than the last blowout. They ended up buying another new tire from the guy, they were not only a tow company but also a tire shop, talk about being lucky.

They were still 10 miles from the border, and one mountain pass to go before they would be out of Colorado. It was late they were both determined to get the hell out of Colorado "Enough is enough!" Frank told Aggie. Then Frank added, I don't know what we did to Colorado, but it sure doesn't like us this time around.

They were only 5 miles away from the border. As they came down the mountain range it started raining. You have to remember they didn't have wipers that worked normally! They called them the crazy wipers, or possessed whichever you prefer. Frank would have to take the fuse out so the wipers wouldn't run, and when he needed to use them he would pull over and put the fuse back in. Sometimes they would work kinda normal and other times they were going every which way. Then other times they would work normal, and then when Frank touch the brakes, they would go crazy. Aggie was very glad that she did not have to drive the RV. Frank drove with no wiper as he headed down the hill, he was determined to get out of Colorado, he had no intention of stopping until them were in Utah.

Aggie had already found an RV campground online. They could stay there for the night; it was at the bottom of the hill. As soon as they crossed the border, the sky turned blue the sun came out, it was the weirdest thing you ever saw.

As they came into the Salina, UT, Aggie was watching out for the campground signs, but she didn't see the one she was looking for. She radioed Frank and told him to turn around at the next exit; she had spotted another campground, which they could go to. They got turned around and headed back into town, this time Aggie took the lead. It was hard to spot things when she followed him. Within a mile, she saw the campground she was looking for; she radioed

Frank and told him to turn at this exit. Are you sure, it looks like a dump. She radioed back; it has a high ranking on their web site. I think it is part of a truck stop. We'll give it a shot, if we don't like it, we'll go to the other one.

Once they stopped Frank asked Aggie, Well what do you think of traveling now? It's an adventure honey!! We made it work, Aggie told him. They both laughed, it was good to be out of Colorado.

CHAPTER 7

Utah

The next day, Aggie called her folk's to let them know they were in Salina, UT. They normally just drive through Salina, but after talking to her parents they suggested they would come to them. After hearing all of their problems, Aggies's mom Grace, figured they needed to take a break. Aggie agreed with her, they were going to come back this way anyway.

Aggie went on line to find out the history of Salina, it's been awhile since she had done any research. This is what she found: "The first permanent settlers (about 30 families) moved into the area in 1864 at the direction of leaders of The Church of Jesus Christ of Latter-day Saints. After finding abundant salt deposits nearby them, they named the area "Salina" because of it. In 1866 troubles with Indians who used the area as their hunting ground forced the white settlers to retreat to the Manti, UT area. They returned to Salina in 1871, organized a militia, and constructed a fort and buildings for a school and a church. They discovered coal deposits in "almost inexhaustible quantities" in the canyon east of the settlement.

Aggie hadn't heard this story before, Frank listens to her read the story, "In Salina during WWII, it housed 250 German prisoners, and they were both from the Wehrmact and the Waffen-SS. On the night of July 8, 1945, Private Clarence Bertucci (an American soldier) climbed one of the guard towers and took aim at the tents where the prisoners were sleeping. He fired rounds from a light machine gun, which was in the guard tower. He managed to hit thirty tents, which the Germans lived in, during his fifteen-second rampage. By the time a corporal managed to disarm Bertucci, six prisoners were dead and an additional twenty-two were wounded (three would later die of their wounds). This incident was called the Salina Massacre. Bertucci, who was from New Orleans, was declared insane and spent the remainder of his life in an institution.

Frank said to Aggie, interesting does it say when he died; I have to wonder why he went nuts like that. Aggie responded, I looked his name up, it looks like he hated Germans, and it sounds like he planned it. It wasn't just a spur of the moment thing. He died in 1969, and in 2016 a museum was built on the site of Camp Salina, with a memorial for the Germans that was killed. We could go see it when the folks get here. I would also like to go to Manti, UT it looks pretty interesting too.

It was a beautiful evening; it was warm and not a cloud in the sky. Frank and Aggie were sitting outside enjoying the night air. Frank had grilled some pork steak, and Aggie made some potatoes salad, and baked beans. It was nice knowing they were going to be there for a couple of days.

They heard a horn honk, which wasn't a big deal, being by the highway. Then they heard it again, this time they looked down the campground road, and Aggie saw her folks, waving at them. It was quite a surprise, they had told Aggie they would be there tomorrow.

Aggie didn't care, she was happy to see them. Her folks pulled up to them, and her Dad, being the funny guy said, "Hey is this spot taken, as he pointed to the spot next to them. Frank replied, yes, you'll have to move on! Everyone laughed, by this time Aggies's folks had gotten out of their truck; there were hugs all around and kisses. Aggie was so happy to see her parents.

After the hello's Frank helped Lazelle, Aggies's father, set up their trailer next to them. Frank carried their lawn chairs over to their site. Frank told them, I have some Lone Star beer, anyone what one? Lazelle and Aggie said yes, and Grace asked do you have any wine? Aggie responded, you bet ya, Frank never leaves home without it. Frank gave her one of his looks, and then said "True, I'll get you a glass, as he disappears into their rig. Aggie asked her parents how was the family. Grace responded, their busy with their life's, we don't see them very much. We tried to get them to come with us, but they had other plans, but they did say Hi! Aggie understood, but she wished they could at least come for the day. It was only a two hour drive, if that. Funny how family say they miss you, yet won't take a break from their life to see them. Aggie was disappointed but that's life. She was just happy her parents could join them.

Aggie told her parents about going to Manti, UT tomorrow and maybe to the museum at the Salina camp. They agreed that would be great, as long as they lived in Utah, they had never been there. The rest of the evening was nice; they talked about the family and what was going on with everyone. Lazelle gave Frank a hard time about having two blow outs in two days. Frank just smiled and took it, that's what father-in-laws do. Grace told Frank, I'm just glad you kept it on the road. Frank told her, me too!

Aggie showed them the flyer they had picked up earlier. "Manti, home of the Mormon Miracle Pageant, is a city of great historical relevance. First settled in 1849, it still has more than 100 buildings that were built by pioneer craftsmen, more than any other city in Utah. Many of these buildings predate the civil war. Because the majority of the builders were stone masons, most of the structures are built of oolite limestone quarried from the hills behind the temple." Grace enjoyed history as much as Aggie did. Aggie figured that was where she got the love for history from.

After a little while Lazelle and Grace headed home, around 11:00 p.m. and told them we will see you around 9, we like to sleep in. As they walked away and waved good-night.

Aggie wanted to check her email before going to bed; Frank was tired so he headed to bed. She got a few emails from her grandkids, telling her about their sports and how they were getting ready for a dance. She also received a letter from Larie', she printed up the emails so Frank could read the letters tomorrow. She was surprised to hear they were already in Delta. The next morning Frank got up before Aggie, she told him she had printed up the emails for him.

Hello Aggie,

I got your email the other day, it sounds like you're having a bad time, can't believe you had two blow outs in two days that's crazy. Didn't you just buy the tires last year, it's weird you only had 3000 miles on them. Well at least you guys didn't get hurt, and Frank was able to pull the RV off the road before something bad happened.

We made it to Riddle, OR, we stayed there for three days. Dean had a great time visiting all the places he used to hang out at when he was 7-8 years old. We stayed in Tri-City, there was a nice RV Campground just outside of town, and we were in the middle of the Valley, it was a wonderful view, and so peaceful. The weather was in the 70s, and NO WIND, it was great. We checked out the cemetery outside of Riddle, it had a lot of Riddle family members. I guess that's why the town is called Riddle! When Dean was living there, the Nickel Mine was the main company, but it slowed down to almost nothing, so now there are Lumber Mills running the town.

Here's a little history for you:

"Riddle was first settled in the mid 1800's by William H. Riddle, a native of Springfield, Illinois. By 1881, the Southern Pacific Railroad line south of Roseburg had a station there called "Riddlesburg", which was changed o "Riddles" in 1880s and to "Riddle" in 1889. There is a post office at this location that was opened under the name "Riddles" in 1882 and was changed to "Riddle" in 1910. Riddle is nestled in one of the many "Valleys of the Umpqua." It was a nickel mining town until the late 1980's, with several square miles of nickel bearing gamierite surface deposits nearby. This was the only nickel mine within the United

States, until it closed for the third and final time in 1998."

Anyway, we were talking about staying here a little longer but we decided we better get going there's another storm front coming. It has been on our tail since we left the coast. I think I told you we want to go to Lakeview, Oregon, to do some rock hounding and check out that area. We haven't been there except to drive through it a couple times, coming from Nevada. So we went down to Ashland, Oregon, and took hwy 60, according to the map it was the shortest way to get there. Boy was that a mistake, as I drove behind Dean, the RV was pitching and rolling back and forth, it was horrible, and I held my breath every time he hit one of those holes. Every time he went to the right, I was afraid he was going to go off the road and over the cliff. As we climb the mountain the road seems to get worse, and then the storm hit us it started raining and as we drove over the mountain it started to snow, what a nightmare. Then it happened a rock flew up and hit the windshield of the car. It went crack, as I looked in the direction of the noise I could see the crack going up the windshield. Then after another mile or so I heard another crack and then I looked to the left and there was two nice size holes/cracks on the other side of the windshield. I ended up backing off from Dean, hoping

not to get any more rocks in the windshield.
By the time we got off the mountain I had
one 5 inch crack and four little cracks on
the windshield. Granted it is not as bad as
a blowout by any means, but it sure sucks
to have cracks in your windshield! So my
recommendation if you come back to Oregon
don't take Highway 60, it really is not made
for RVs to go over.

We found this really nice little
campground outside of Lakeview and
originally we were planning on spending
just one day but after Hwy 60, we decided
to stay a couple of days and check out the
town. A little history about Lakeview, it was
established in 1876, with an elevation of
4798 feet. Lakeview is often referred to as
the "Tallest Town in Oregon". Lakeview is
situated at the foot of the Warner Mountains
and at the edge of southeast Oregon High
Desert". The town was name Lakeview,
because of the excellent view of Goose Lake
which you can see from the town site, at that
time".

There were only four RVs at the park and
two of them were empty. The guy that ran
the place had only purchased the business
two years ago and was trying to improve it.
It seems like most of the RV campgrounds
have new owners these days. What was
really weird is there was a geyser on the next
property. When we first saw it we thought a

water line must have busted or something. But then we saw it again and again so we decided it had to be something different. We could see the stream of water coming up in the distance, in the beginning we really didn't know what it was, until we asked the owner about it. He said, "It's "Old Perpetual" it's the only active hot water geyser in the Pacific Northwest. The geyser spouts a plume of 200° hot water over 60 feet in the air about every minute. It's called Hunter's hot spring resort; it has an outdoor hot mineral pool with the temperature of 104°. But it's closed for the winter he told us." I was kinda bummed, I rather like the idea of soaking in the hot water but what can you do?

We ended up's waking up the next morning to 2 inches of new snow; it was a good thing that we had decided to stay another day. This seems to be our theme we drive someplace and get snow. But we are getting closer hopefully to sunny weather. There are a couple of mines here that we would've liked to go dig in, but everything was still closed for the winter, nothing opens up until 1 May. So I guess we'll have to come back again, but this time we will not take Highway 60!

The snow was gone before noon, so we decided to go to California. There was a little town on the OR/CA border which was only 15 miles away; we had no plans of going to CA this trip. We found a nice little hamburger place in town, it was called Queen Burgers. The town is a lot bigger than we first thought we ended driving around the town, which didn't take long to explore. There were a lot of old big homes and old buildings which I always enjoy looking at, but then that's normal for old Oregon towns.

We've been traveling like you suggested: 2 x 2 x 2, drive two hours, drive 200 miles, and stay at least two days at each location. So far it's working out great; we ended up east of Winnemucca, Nevada next, it was a brand-new RV campground. It also had many cabins that were lined up, end to end. Each of the cabins had three bedrooms and three baths for the miner's and construction workers, which come in during the summer. There had to be at least a 100 of them just lined up, row after row of them. There was also a nice little casino at the campground and a restaurant. We only stayed two nights then we headed off to your hometown Delta, Utah.

We were bummed that we didn't get to see you guys while we were there. We did have a good time; we went fossils hunting out at the place you suggested. We found trilobites they were small from a dime to a quarter sizes. But the guy there was really interesting; I didn't know there were so many different types. We also went to the two museums in town; there were a lot of things to see. We'll be heading to Grand Junction next to see Dean's sister, she is the one that is living in an assisted living home. She has MS in her brain; it's been awhile since we have seen her. It'll be nice to see her. Well hopefully, everything is going better for you guys. I'll be looking forward to your next letter.

As always, Larie'

Frank made coffee and picked up the emails to read, while Aggie slept in. He went and sat outside, it was a beautiful morning, it was a little chilly, but with a jacket on it was just right. As he drank his coffee and went thru the emails, he could hear Aggie moving around inside. He had just finished reading all the email, when Aggie stepped out of the RV. Morning sleepy head, did you have another bad night, Frank asked her. She smiled, yeah, but it's all good. Did you read all the emails? Yea, Larie' sure likes to write Huh? Aggie smiled, and said don't we all, you should see the letters I write her. It sounds like their enjoying their new found freedom. Frank agreed, and then he heard, Morning fellow traveler!

It was Aggie folks, and it looked like they were ready to do some traveling. Lazelle had a small ice chest in hand and Grace had the picnic basket and their jackets just in case it gets cold. Lazelle said, "Let's go we are burning daylight!" Aggie had a flashback on how many times she had heard that in her childhood.

Aggie looked at Frank, and told him, well let's get a move on. Aggie told everyone the first stop is Manti, UT it's not that far; it's only 27 miles away. Frank said, I'm on it, he went inside and opened some windows and turned on the fans for the girls. He made sure there was lots of water and food for them. It was much better for them to stay home then sit in the car while they walked around the town. While Frank was doing that Aggie put water and fruit in their basket, her mom said she had lunch covered.

Then they loaded up and headed south, in no time at all they were in Manti, UT. They stopped at the Historic Manti City Hall, which was the visitor center too. The sign read, "The building was an early Italianate design, which was built between 1873 and 1882 as the city could afford it. It ended up costing the city $1,100, which is really a good deal considering how large the house was." The brochure that they picked up at City Hall had houses that they suggested as a walking tour. It sounded good to them!

The brochure had 29 houses listed, with a little bit of history on each of the houses. They decide to start with Manti Temple; it was quite impressive it's stood at the north entrance to the city. They walked around the grounds and then walked over to the cemetery afterwards, which was across from the Temple. "Many of the earlier settlers were buried in the cemetery. Most of the older graves are in the central part of the cemetery. There were quite a few gravestones of babies and young children. According to the brochure there are graves of pioneers who were killed by the Indians and even some Indians were buried there."

They walked from building to building and were amazed at the architecture and the designs of the different buildings. They walked over to the beach log cabin. Lazelle told them, this looks like the cabin I was raised in. Grace told him well at least you live in a better house now! He smiled at her, and replied how true. They started to get hungry, so they stopped at the city's park and had a picnic lunch.

It ended up being a beautiful day so they were able to see most of the houses. But after walking around all morning, Lazelle and Grace started getting tired, so they decided to take the car to do the rest of the tour. They headed back to the campground around 1p.m., on the way home they saw a herd of buffalos in a field. Lazelle said, "That's a healthy looking herd, look at all the calves." Frank responded, It pretty cool seeing herd of buffalos out there in the field. I bet it was something to see 1000s of them roaming the fields in the old days.

Frank suggested they still had time to go to Camp Salina; it's not far from the campground. They all agreed it would be interesting to see. They stopped by the RV, and took the girls out for a quick walk and then headed over to the Camp Salina. The camp restoration was started in Dec 2014 and still going on. Some of the building had already been restored; but there was still work to be done. So far there was some barracks, and houses. They had a display of what the Camp looked like during their hay day. It was originally a CCC Camp. There was also a film they watched, it had interviews from a couple of the Germans that were imprisoned for several years there. Aggie told Frank, this place reminds me of the Ft. Jackson, TX and a few of the other camps built in the 40s. It was a hard life back then, with no air condition, and only a wood burning stove.

It was very interesting; these guys had it made compared to the way our soldiers were treated in Europe, Lazelle told Frank. Frank had to agree, he had visited some of the places in Germany where they held our soldiers, and they were not even close to this place. Even the German soldiers had to agree, they didn't have that much comfort at the end of the War either.

Aggies's Dad, Lazelle had been in Germany during WWII and had been in five major campaigns, he wasn't too fond of the German. This was understandable; he had lost friends, and saw a lot of terrible things during the war. He wasn't one to talk about the hell he lived through during those years. But every once in awhile he would tell Frank some of the things that he had seen. He showed Frank a spike he had in his nightstand, he told Frank he was driving down an old Germany road when he hit the spike. He could tell by the style of the spike it had fallen off of a German engineer truck. This was the third flat tire he had gotten that day, so he wasn't too happy to get another one. The spike was really jammed into the tire. As he was pulling the spike out of the tire, it came out with a jolt and went into his leg. There wasn't much he could do, but cursed that thing as he pulled it out. The good news was that it didn't get any major blood vessels. He bandaged it as good as he could and headed on his way. As far as he was concerned, if that was the worst that could happen to him, he was in good shape.

They went back to the campground and Frank got the BBQ started, and Grace went back to their trailer and came back with a fruit salad. They settled in and had dinner, then played some cards, and planned their following travels.

Aggie pulled out the Utah map, where she had drawn a line on places she thought it would be fun to go. She laid the map out on the table and said first stop Arches National Park.

It was always interesting to go there and see if any more Arches have collapsed. They have been going there for 55 years; every summer Aggies's family would go camping up in the mountains. Aggie loved the history and the stories she would hear about the area.

Here's a little history of Arches National Park that she had found online. "Native Americans utilized the area for thousands of years. Archaic people, and later ancestral Puebloan, Fremont and Utes searched the arid desert for game animals, wild plant foods and stone for tools and weapons. They also left evidence of their passing on a few pictograph and petroglyphs panels."

They used to visit the Wolfe Ranch; it was like walking into the past. "The first white explorers came looking for wealth in the form of minerals. Ranchers found wealth in the grasses for their cattle and sheep. John Wesley Wolfe, a disabled Civil War veteran, and his son, Fred, settled here in the late 1800s. A weathered log cabin, root cellar and a corral remain as evidence of the primitive ranch they operated for more than 20 years."

"Paleo-Indians lived in the lush canyons leading to the Green and Colorado rivers from about 10,000 to 7,800 BC and might have been the earliest people to see the Arches. Although there is no evidence of Paleo-Indian use in the park, their spear points and camps have been found nearby."

"By 9,000 years ago, the climate here became too warm and dry for many large mammals. The mammals and some of the Paleo-Indian hunters moved to higher habitats. Those who stayed in the canyon country depended more on gathering and traveling. This lifestyle, called Archaic, meant that the people had to live in small groups and travel extensively. Archaeologists have found a few spear points, occasional campsites, and quarries for stone needed to make tools. Barrier Canyon style rock art panels, once attributed to the more recent Fremont culture, are the best evidence of the Archaic hunter-gathers in Arches."

This is only a small part of its history, but the next time you're in the park, it will be a little more interesting. Most people don't read the signs as they travel around the park.

Aggie turned to her Dad and told him next stop Wilson Arch, are you going to run to the top like you have always done. Lazelle responded, "I think I'm getting a little old for that, but you never know!" Aggie just laughed and said, I guess we'll see. After that we can set up camp at the RV Campground we stayed in a few years ago in Moab. From there we can go to Bluff and Mexican Hat, and visit some of the cousins while there. Grace spoke up and said, it sounds like you have been planning this for a little while. Aggie just smiled, and said "Living the Dream!"

The next morning they got up and started packing things up and getting ready to leave, they figured they would leave around 10 a.m. they were in no big hurry. Frank and Agatha took the lead, and headed down I70. Frank radioed to Agatha and told her I forgot how beautiful it is a long I70. The red rocks, and the way the rocks are shaped is just amazing. It's hard to keep my eyes on the road, Aggie could hear Frank laugh. Aggie responded back, Utah definitely has a lot of colors, even just the different shades of red. With the river running along the road just adds to the amazing view and the beauty of this area.

They arrived at the Arches and parked the RV's in the parking lot by the main gate and took the Jeep into the park. They stopped at a couple of the pull offs, where they have stopped many times before. There were a couple of arches that had fallen, other than that nothing much had changed. It was as beautiful as always. After doing a little bit of hiking and checking out the area they headed back to the RV. They arrived back at the parking lot where they had parked the RV earlier.

There was a tour bus full of Japanese tourists and they were taking pictures of Penelope, their RV. Aggie told Frank well I guess Penelope is going to be a star in Japan! Frank laughed and said I guess. Once they pulled up to Penelope they all smiled and waved at them and got back on the tour bus.

They loaded up and headed down the road to Wilson Arch. "Wilson Arch, also known as Wilson's Arch, is a natural sandstone arch in Southeastern Utah, just off U.S.191. It has a span of 91 feet and height of 46 feet. The Arch is visible from the road to the east where there are turnouts with interpretive signs. The elevation of Wilson Arch is about 6,150 feet (1,870 m)."

It didn't take long to get there. They pulled off the road into the turnout; it is a little pull off where people can park and go check out the arch. They added a sign since the last time Aggie and Frank were there. According to the sign, "Wilson Arch was named after Joe Wilson, a local pioneer who had a cabin nearby in Dry Valley. This formation is known as Estrada Sandstone. Over time superficial cracks, joints, and folds of these layers were saturated with water. Ice formed in the fissures, melted under extreme desert heat, and winds cleaned out the loose particles. A series of free-standing fins remained. Wind and water attacked these fins until, in some, cementing material gave way and chunks of rock tumbled out. Many damaged fins collapsed like the one to the right of Wilson Arch. Others, with the right degree of hardness survived despite their missing their middle like Wilson Arch."

As Aggie was reading the sign out loud, she turned and saw her dad running up the hill to the arch, it was quite the surprise. Not to be outdone Frank took off after him. Of course, Aggie and her mom had to do the same. They all were under the arch and looking out over the valley, it is quite a view from up there. Lazelle turned to Aggie and said "I bet you didn't think I could do it!" Aggie smiled and said; of course I knew you could do it. Then she asked him if he was doing okay. He laughed and said yeah. As they headed down the hill, Frank said I think it's harder to go down the hill, they all had to agree with him it was pretty steep hill.

Next stop Moab; they had made it in no time at all. They set up camp; they had made reservations to go on the evening boat ride. As usual it didn't take long to set up camp, and they were going to have dinner at the Canyon Lands Night Dinner Cruise. After dinner they were going to take the cruise.

They got there just in time for dinner, it was a cowboy-style dinner, and it was amazing. They were glad they saved their appetite, there was so much to eat; there was pulled pork and BBQ beef, juicy corn, and homemade rolls.

They climbed aboard the Moab Queen II, which was a flat-bottomed boat, and it was going to take them three-miles up the Colorado River. The boat was a little loud, but the guide would stop and talk about the area. He talked about the settlement of the area, interesting and unique facts about the region, and the different formation of the rocks around them. As they were going down the river a Blue Heron decided to race the boat. The Heron won, Frank saw it again standing on the river bank, and well he thought it might be the same one. It was looking at the boat as if saying I won.

It took a little over three hours, for everything, it was great! The flyer said; "The terrain is full of some of the wildest natural landscapes across American" they were right! One nice thing about "Moab it is conveniently located between Canyonlands National Park, Arches National Park, and Dead Horse State Park, all of which are important American landmarks for Moab visitors to explore. This area is so inspiring that this cruise has been ongoing for more than 50 years!"

We ended back at the dock and once it got dark, the natural starlight lite up the canyon walls, revealing the majestic beauty of the land which inspired settlers and Native Americans alike. With the aid of lights, shadows, music, and narration, they listened to the stories about the formation, creation, and history of the area from the early settlers. "Because the park is so isolated, it allows a stunning view of the stars and the Milky Way glowing high above." It was a great time, but it was time to head back to the RV. They arrived back at their RV's and let the dogs out. All the way back they talked about everything they saw and heard. Grace told Aggie that was something else wasn't it, Aggie had to agree and so did the guys. They said their good nights and planned on leaving to the Bluff area tomorrow. They wanted to leave early because they wanted to go to Mexican Hat to see Grace's sister and family.

Aggie couldn't help it she got on line to see what to look for while they were out tomorrow. According to the Bluff web site, there was a lot of history in the area.

"Ancient artifacts and rock art discovered in the vicinity of the Bluff Valley go back to the days of mammoth hunters. The hunting-and-gathering mode of life held sway for about 8,500 years as small groups of people moved in and out of the region. With the introduction of corn-based agriculture, the pace of social change dramatically quickened. Around AD 600 the first apparent farming community in the valley was established in the sand dunes on the west side of modern Bluff.

These people lived in houses that dotted the terraces above and along the San Juan River; they grew corn, squash, and newly introduced beans; and they made the first real pottery, which made possible the cooking of beans. Archaeological investigation of this community has revealed such public facilities as a cemetery and a great kiva."

Just in case you don't know what an Indian Kiva is: "A kiva is a room used by Puebloans for religious rituals and political meetings, many of them associated with the kachina belief system. Among the modern Hopi and most other Pueblo peoples, kivas are square-walled and underground, and are used for spiritual ceremonies." Frank said to Aggie, "there are similar subterranean rooms among ruins in the American Southwest, remember the ones we saw in Arizona? For the Ancestral Puebloans, it's believed the room had a variety of functions, including domestic residence along with social and ceremonial purposes. Aggie told him yes, it's funny there so far apart but still have the basic same living style.

"Twin Rocks is a striking rock formation on the east side of modern Bluff. People of this time period clustered together into blocks of rooms and pithouses. These villagers introduced red ware pottery, including a pottery type that archaeologists named for its first place of recognition: Bluff Black-on-red.

Little formal investigation of this site has occurred; however, a large portion of this ancient pueblo is now protected by local nonprofit organizations. A century later, the pendulum of social importance swung to the south side of the river to a site known as "Dance Plaza". A large rectangular room, or "dance plaza," is the main feature on the site. Nearby, a pair of large boulders tower over the plaza."

"The Mesa Verde region includes the canyon-rich landscapes of southeastern Utah. Arriving from New Mexico, this "Chacoan Phenomenon" featured bold architectural elements: great houses, great kivas, and roads. Bluff Valley's social center was relocated to the north side of the river onto a hilltop that overlooks the entire valley. At the Bluff Great House site, were a multi-story masonry great house and an enormous subterranean great kiva. Archaeological research suggests that the site remained in use for about 200 years. The site itself was the southern terminus of an extensive network of great houses and prehistoric roads that stretched from the San Juan River to the foot of the Abajo Mountains in the north. By the mid-1,200s, this great alliance had fallen apart, and the Puebloan people moved south to inhabit the landscapes of the Rio Grande, the Zuni Mountains, and the Hopi Mesas."

Aggie was always amazed how much you can find on line, otherwise they wouldn't know about all the things there is to see, and the wonderful history of our country. She printed it up and went into the bedroom and read it to Frank. He told her, sounds interesting, looking forward to exploring it tomorrow. Did your Mom call her sister and let her know we'll be in Mexican Hat tomorrow? Aggie told him yes, and they are looking forward to seeing us all.

It didn't take long for them to fall asleep, they were up by 6 and her folks were there at 7, they didn't want to burn too much day light. The dogs were set up for the day, food and water and the fans turn on. They still wanted to explore the Moab area, so they left the RV in the Moab campground. Bluff was a little over 100 miles away, and then another twenty-five miles to Mexican Hat, UT.

They loaded up and headed down the road. Aggie drove, and her Mom rode in front with her, and the guys rode in the back. It may have been a hundred miles, but it didn't feel that way to any of them. There was non-stop talking. When they arrived in Bluff, they found a place to eat, they went to Twin Rock Café, the food was great, and after they ate they headed over to the Bluff Fort.

They stopped at the visitors' center, and then they went into the museum grounds. As they roamed around all the cabins and exhibits, and learning the stories of the pioneers who settled Bluff. The folks responsible for putting this center together did an absolutely first-rate job! Aggie wished the grandkids could see this museum. The kids would love it; they loved history as much as she did. They would love all the covered wagons they could climb up into and the wooden horses they could sit on. "Great way to appreciate the history of the early Anglo settlers of Bluff; the headstones for several of the people mentioned at the fort are located in the cemetery above town; just down the road from the cemetery is a small Chacoan archaeological site.

The story about the "The Hole-in-the-Rock", was remarkable. There was a Memorial to "Honor the men, women and children of the San Juan Mission who came to the area in 1880 in answer to a call from their church."

"These Mormon pioneers over came challenges of unparallel difficulty as they blazed a road through some of the most broken and rugged terrain in North America. Including a path through the Colorado River Gorge via a crevice they that was only surpassed by formidable task of settling the San Juan frontier."

As they wandered around, Grace, Aggies's mom, was talking about the hardships her family had lived thru in Oklahoma, but nothing as bad as this. Her family had moved from Oklahoma when she was a teenager, she was the youngest of 12 kids. Her older brothers had written her parents that Durango, Colorado was a great place to live and there were no tornados, in that part of the state.

Her parents had enough of the tornados in Oklahoma; they had been hit twice and pretty much lost everything the last time around. Aggie loved the story about how her Grandparent's pulled up to the farm where the boys were, and there were human skulls on every fence post. The boys had discovered an Indian graveyard, and picked up the bones. Her Grandmother started yelling at the boys, to get the skulls off the fence posts and put them back where they found them. She refused to get out of the car until they were all removed. Aggie could only imagine how it would be to drive up to your property and see human skulls on the fence post.

They went over and looked at the petroglyphs, at the base of the enormous boulders and saw two holes. According to the sign; "The two large deeply pecked holes, may have represented the Puebloan *sipapu* or place of emergence."

As they were heading back to the car, Frank pointed out to the group; it is interesting how many places have petroglyphs. In our travels we have seen them in AZ, CO, UT, NM and many more places. They are a little different in each region, but yet the same. There is always some type of people and animals in the petroglyphs. Aggie agreed, what is really amazing that they are still there. Everyone had to agree, it was getting late, and they wanted to still go to Mexican Hat to visit Grace's sister. Grace called her sister from the car, and they agreed they would meet at Swing Steak Café. That sounded good to Aggie and Frank, they never turned down steak.

On the way to Mexican Hat, they talked about the plans for tomorrow; they were going to hang out around the Moab area. They really have been enjoying their time together.

Grace's sister called her, and told her they were inside and already had a table, so just come on in. Frank parked the Jeep, and they headed into the café, it was an open sided café, so they saw their family right away. After the hugs and hellos were done, they had to go over and check out the BBQ. It was a large grill that swings back and forth. The cook put the large steak on the grill; it takes about 20 minutes for a medium rare steak to be cooked. The steaks were amazing; the meal came with the salad and beans. There is nothing like good company and amazing steak. Aggie was enjoying watching her mom visit with her sister. They were reminiscing about when they were kids and old friends they had. But it was getting late and they needed to get back to the dogs.

Aggie found out a little more about Mexican Hat, it's a great location to visit of the many parts of Utah. "Mexican Hat is a tiny desert community of 50 or so people near the southeastern corner of Utah. It sits along the San Juan River among impressive rock formations. In fact, Mexican Hat itself gets its name from a rock formation north of town that resembles an overturned sombrero. The town serves mainly as a stopping off point for those traveling to Monument Valley (22 miles southwest) and Natural Bridges National Monument (44 miles north). Mexican Hat is also a convenient base for those exploring the San Juan River."There are so many other things to see within an15 mile ratios from town: Goosenecks State Park, Muley Point Overlook and the Valley of the Gods.

"Goosenecks State Park frames slow, dramatic bends in the San Juan River, bends that have slowly eroded deep canyons in the stone. Muley Point Overlook also deals with the San Juan, allowing the visitor to stare over less dramatic, but plentiful and winding canyons. Valley of the Gods is far dryer, a series of carved buttes and pinnacles reminiscent of the larger Monument Valley."

Aggie told Frank maybe we can do a vacation here with the kids next year. Aggies's folks told her just let us know and we'll join you. Aggie was smiling and said how great that would be; maybe my brother and sister can take a little time away from home. Frank laughed and said we'll have to reserve the whole RV campground here.

The rest of the ride home was quiet, Aggies parents fell asleep, for a little bit. They arrived home around 8 p.m., the girls were happy to see them, and were ready to get out of the RV. Their friend came over and said, she took them to her place for a little while, but they wanted to come home. So she put them back in the RV around 6. Frank smiled and said thanks and they walked her back to her RV and then continued on walking the girls. Their folks said good night and headed back to their rig. We'll see you around 9 tomorrow. Sounds like a plan, Frank told them.

After they walked the girls, they headed to bed themselves. It was a great day, but a lot of walking. It didn't take them long to fall asleep. The next morning they met up with the folks and headed over to the Dinosaur stomping ground and then checked out the museum.

As they walked around the area, Frank was saying, it is interesting to see tracks in the rocks that were made by Dinosaurs; but it is weird that something like that would still be here after all these years. They wandered around for a little while longer checking out the area and then they decided to head over to the Dinosaur museum in town.

After hiking around the mountain, it was nice to get inside a building. It was a small museum about the history of the town of Moab and nearby areas. It had a lot of interesting stuff. They have fossilized dinosaur prints and bones. It also had Native American pottery, baskets, baby carrier, arrows, dolls and a stunning quilt. It was nice it was small and it only cost five dollars. After the museum they headed home, the folks wanted to go take a nap, and Aggie and Frank took the girls out for a walk. They stopped at the office, and checked out the flyer they had for the area. Then they went back to the RV. Frank decided a nap sounded good so he went and lay down, and the girls were right behind him.

Aggie sat outside until the mosquitoes started attacking her. She is allergic to them and she wasn't looking forward to the welts she was about to get. By the time that she got into the RV they had already started swelling. All she could think of was those Damn mosquitoes! She was enjoying the evening air.

Later on that evening the folks came over and had dinner, and talked about the day they had. They all agreed they enjoyed being together for the last two weeks. But it was time to head back to Texas, and Aggies's parents needed to get to the farm.

Aggies's parents asked them, "Where are you guys headed next?" Aggie told them, well the plan is to go east, hang out in Texas for a little bit and then go into Arkansas, then Tennessee and who knows where from there. Frank told them one thing for sure we're not going to Colorado again, we don't want the road gremlins attacking us again, and he smiled and laughed. Aggie had to agree with him, Colorado was not on their list of places to go right now. She said it's been nice having everything going great; it's been wonderful hanging out with you guys. It's been more like hanging out with good friends and your parents at the same time. Aggie suggested to them that she would make breakfast in the morning, do you want to come over around 8, if that's okay. Her folks said, "Sounds great see you then!"

That evening Aggie looked at the maps trying to figure out which direction they would be going. She asked Frank what you think about going down to New Mexico and stopping at Raton, NM. A little farther than we normally drive but I think it'll be okay. Frank said that will be fine, you know me I'm always willing to get back to Texas as fast as I can!

The next morning the folks came over for breakfast and they said their goodbyes. Aggie told them to give us a call when you get home so we know you made it okay! They agreed and headed back to the rig, and headed down the road. Aggie turned to Frank and said it's been great spending time with them hopefully we can do it again. Frank had to agree it was really a pleasant time. They definitely got around for as old as they are, I hope we can keep up with them when we're their age. Aggie walked back and got into the Jeep and Frank got into Penelope. They headed down the road toward New Mexico. Aggie radioed Frank and said "Look out Texas here we come!"

CHAPTER 8

New Mexico

As much as they didn't want to run into the Colorado gremlins, it made more sense to go to the lower part of Colorado to New Mexico. The plan was to stop in Chama, NM for the night and then head to Raton, NM. They had not been in the upper part of the New Mexico before; it should be an interesting ride. They figured they had replaced all the tires on Penelope and changed the oil, and got anything else they could make sure there would be no problems before they headed into Colorado. Aggie told Frank it's kind of funny to spend so much time in Colorado as a kid growing up now we dread going there.

It was nice going though Colorado this time, they went to Cortez, and visited with their friends for lunch, got talked into staying the night. Frank enjoyed talking to Fred about the good old days. That evening they walked over to the bowling alley and played a couple of games, and had a few beers. It was nice to walk back to the campground; it was a warm evening, with a slight breeze. They said their goodbyes that night because Frank and Aggie wanted to be on their way first thing in the morning.

Fred and Judy told them about the train ride in Chama, NM it's a beautiful ride, little expensive but it worth every penny. Cumbres & Toltec Scenic railroad is a "National Historic Landmark, it is a 64-mile day trip. The coal-fired steam engine carries you through steep mountain canyons, high desert, and lush meadows as you zig zag between the Colorado and New Mexico border. It's has spectacular and rare Western scenery which can only be viewed from the train's unique route."

Frank suggested to Aggie they should do it. He reminded her of the last time they took a train ride was out of Durango, CO. We took the kids and stopped at that old mine. The kids had a great time. Aggie agreed with him, it was a lot of fun. She told him Chama sounds like an interesting place to stay for a few days. She had found a campground that sounds pretty nice too.

As usual Aggie had to look up the information about Chama, and read it to Frank. It is another town that came to life with the railroad. "In February 1880, the Denver and Rio Grande Railroad began construction of the San Juan extension, a route that went from Alamosa, CO to Silverton, CO by way of Cumbres Pass, Chama and Durango. Railroad service to Chama began in February, 1881 and facilities for servicing railroad equipment, a depot, warehouses and stockyards were set up along the route surveyed for the railroad." Aggie told Frank I think this is part of the ride we took from Durango, he had to agree.

She continued to read, "Chama had a brief construction period from 1880-1881 which was the most exciting episodes in the area's history and immediately became a boomtown. Other industrious and disreputable characters came from all around. The development of coal mines in Monero rapidly appeared, and lumber industry, laborers, engineers and contractors to build the railroad."

The story goes, "For many years Chama remained a rowdy and exciting place to be. It was a very prosperous town with plenty of work and a great deal of entertainment in the forms of saloons, gambling houses, moonshine stills, etc. Groceries were very expensive and outlaws, such as the Clay Allison gang. He regularly held up the railroad pay car and construction camps because they had large payrolls, saloons and gambling houses."

Sounds like it was a wild place at one time, Frank told Aggie! Yeah, listen to this part. "In the past, the main industries of the area were logging, mining and sheep and cattle ranching. Before the logging industry clear-cut much of the timber, the vast grasslands one now sees, were hundreds of square miles of forest. In pre-logging days the forest was so thick that it was difficult for a man on a horseback to negotiate his way through the trees. The sheep industry operated on a grand scale until the depression and the terrible winter of 1931-32 combined to nearly wipe out the sheep industry.

It sounds like they had a lot of hardship there, Aggie told Frank. He agreed it'll be interesting to check it out. It is nice learning a little history about a town before visiting it; it really does make a difference. Aggie agreed, it is great having the internet, I don't know how people traveled before. She smiled at Frank; he replied back, we didn't do too badly before the internet. Aggie smiled back at him, Yeah, we did find some interesting places.

They arrived at Chama around 1 p.m., there wasn't much to set up camp, and they left everything in the Jeep, and moved the buckets under the RV. They took the girls for a walk and checked out the campground, it was a nice place; it was called Rio Chama RV Park. It is located just down the street from the scenic railway about a quarter of a mile.

The owner said a lot of the folks that stay here go on the Cumbres & Toltec rail journey. The park is within a short walk from the station, and you can see the train go by next to the park twice a day. There was no rain in the forecast so they opted for a riverfront space. Frank and Aggie were completely delighted with the location, the river was high and flowing fast, which added to the ambience. The front of their RV was literally 4 ft from the water. It was nice; there was plenty of shade in most of the spots, but not so much on the river front sites. They were happy they stopped there. They purchased the train tickets online for the morning ride, and then they walked around town. It looked like the Old West town, the rowdiness was gone, as far as they could tell, but the town looked like a very cool place to visit.

The next morning they took their girls out for a long walk, and set them up for the day, then headed over to the train depot. It felt like a flash from the past, back to 1880's, being on the stream train. They walked up to the train and handed the ticket to the train conductor and found a seat in one of the train cars. The train whistles blowing and you could hear the steam being released as it jolted forward. It didn't take long to get to the beautiful scenery, they went through the Canyon lands and into the prairies it was remarkable. Aggie couldn't help wondering how they put some of these railroad tracks down; there was just enough room for the train to get through. If they had an earthquake that would be the end of them! The train is followed by a fire car just in case an ember might start something - just like the old days.

The train climbed up to 10,000 ft above sea level very slowly; they said the max speed was 12 mph. The Cumbres & Toltec Railroad is extremely generous with snacks, and free non alcoholic drinks.

They had lunch half way through the trip at Osier, which was a large wooden building. It was a great lunch; they had fresh turkey, and salad bar. It was just like Thanksgiving dinner, Frank told Aggie. Aggie responded, it's better, if you remember our last Thanksgiving.

According to the employee, "The steam engine was a 1924 vintage engine with immense pulling traction. The track is narrow, three feet wide. The route has many, many tight curves, one that is 20 degrees. Leaning out the window you'll get many great photos and videos of the train in operation. Top speed is about 20 mph. Until the mid 1960s the railroad was a freight train hauling oil drilling supplies from Antonito to Chama. The history of this railroad goes back into the 1880s. The scenery is dramatic because of the change from high desert to high mountains (10,000 feet) to high plateau. The train and area around Antonito was used in the filming of Indiana Jones."

They went to the open train car; it kind of looked like a train car that was cut in half. It probably wouldn't be a good place to be on a rainy day, but it was a beautiful day so they enjoyed the fresh air. They stood and looked at the scenery for awhile, then went back to their seats. It was a three hour ride but it went by quickly, part of the tour was to take a tour bus back to Chama. It was only an hour ride back. It is a nice 64 mile scenic trip up from Chama to Antonito, there was some incredible landscapes.

They got off the bus at the train depot when they got back, then they walked back to their RV. The girls were in the window waiting for them. As usual they were ready to go out for their evening walk. As they were walking around the campground, they were going to let them play in the dog park. There was a large white German shepherd already in there. The couple said he was friendly, so they took the girls in to meet him; his name was Bud, and what a sweetheart.

The girls fell in love with him. The couples names were Jill and Keith, they were from Oregon. Aggie told them they had been there and it was a beautiful state. A little more rain than they like, but she guessed that's why they have so many huge trees.

As they talked, Aggie told them that they had taken the Cumbres & Toltec train ride earlier that day, and how remarkable it was. Jill responded I'm glad you guys had a great time. Aggie told her yes it was beautiful countryside. Jill told her that they had been on a train ride a few weeks ago, in Oregon and it was the ride from hell.

Once we arrived the conductor announced there will be buses to take us to our hotel. When we did arrive, they had us stay on the train an extra hour. Why I have no idea.

By then we just wanted to go to our hotel, it was now 11:30. They also told us some of the restaurants agreed to stay open for everyone and they would stay open until midnight. We finally got off the train and there were buses waiting there, but they told us they weren't taking passengers. There were all these buses just parked in the parking lot, but they weren't taking any passengers. They didn't give us any reason, so Keith called a cab. It came right away, thank goodness. Jill squeeze Keith's arm and said "My hero!"

We finally got to our room, but we were still hungry, we decided to find a place to eat. We went next door and waited in line for a half hour and were told that they were closing. Ahhh... And now we were really hungry. The hostess told us there was a Shari's that was open 24/7 and was two blocks down the street. Now Bend isn't a small town so a block is a mile long. So Keith called another cab. She smiled and said, "Life is good when you are full and you can finally hit the pillow."

Aggie replied, I bet! So how was your trip back, Aggie asked? As Jill took a deep breath, WELL we got up the next morning and had a great breakfast at the hotel. We got up early again, around 6:45 a.m. We didn't want to miss the bus. The bus was late and it picked us up at 8:30 a.m. It was around 9:30 am when we boarded the train. Because they didn't turn the train around the night before they had to do it that morning. Of course, that meant we were behind schedule again, it took them an hour to turn the train around.

So we were finally on our way back and had been traveling for about an hour, when they pulled the train over and stopped. It was so hot in the train that a woman had heat stroke. They still had not fixed the air-conditioning in the cars. They had to stop the train and let on paramedics, the paramedics ended up taking her off the train. This took a couple of hours. Which put us off the schedule again; we couldn't believe it was happening again. We finally got to Portland tired and hungry around Midnight. Of course there were no restaurants in the area that were open except McDonalds. Even that tasted so good thou!

Aggie had to agree with her it sounded like it was the ride from hell. At least it wasn't you guys having the heart attack or stroke. Jill had to agree that was true. It was getting late so they headed home. The dogs were just lying next to each other in the dog park; Aggie figured they were just bored. They said good-night to Jill and Keith; they told them that they were heading back to Oregon. Aggie told them "Safe travels" and Jill replied back you too.

The next morning they headed off to Raton, NM, they should be there around 1:00 pm, if everything goes well. Aggie came up with a little back ground on the town. Raton NM is an interesting place, "The town of Raton is cupped at the foot of a 75-mile long volcanic ridge known as the Raton Range, at the nexus of New Mexico's high plains and the eastern edge of the Sangre de Cristo Mountains. It was a stop along the Santa Fe Trail, born during the United States' westward expansion in the middle of the 19th century."

"From the beginning, Raton was a town of immigrants. Italian, Irish, Mexican, Russian, Scottish, Greek and Yugoslavian miners flocked there to dig coal. "Most of the people there grew up in Raton, their ancestors came to mine coal," city manager Scott Berry said. "There were a lot of coal mining towns in the area and they all needed labor. They came from everywhere."

The trip to Raton was beautiful; it was a lot like the scenery they saw on the train. Aggie from heard the campground online. Which was on the highway, they were only going to stay one night, but nothing was in writing. They couldn't miss it, there was a large sign pointing to it. As Aggie was driving by she radioed Frank and told him that is the place on the right. Frank radioed back, it looks like a junkyard. Aggie laughed and said it's after the junkyard. Let's check it out, it's only one night. Frank radioed back to her, Ok.

Aggie was in the lead, it didn't look to bad once they got to the park. They checked in, the owner was very friendly, and told them where to park and off they went to set up for the night. They had heard on the radio that a storm front was coming in, and there could be snow. The owner suggested that they turn the water off at night, so it didn't freeze. It doesn't take too much to freeze a garden hose.

After they set up, they drove around town; it had some beautiful old homes, all sitting empty. Aggie told Frank, there was a lot of money here at one time. It's sad to see them all in disarray. Downtown was almost all closed down, but the buildings were still in great shape.

It started snowing so they headed back to the RV, took the girls for a walk, and settled in for the night. Sage still wanted to play, so she would attack Susi, and pulled her ear, and then Susi would open her mouth and act like she was going to bite her. It was fun to watch them tussle with each other.

That evening the weather came in from the West, first it was heavy winds, and then the snow started. Light at first, and then heavier, and then it started going sideways. They were both glad that they weren't driving in it. Slowly the winds settled down, but the snow was still coming down. Frank turned to Aggie, and said maybe we'll stay another day. If it is snowing like this, you can only imagine how bad it is on the mountain. Yeah, we're in no big hurry, that's the nice thing about being retired. As they headed off to bed, there was only an inch of snow. They were glad they turned off the water earlier, they were pretty sure the hose would be frozen.

The next morning there was three inches of snow on the ground, which wasn't a big deal, but they heard on the news there was a foot of new snow on the mountain. They both agreed they wanted to see a little more of the town anyway. They went over to the office to extend another night. The owner's mother was working the desk. She was in her 70's and had been there for over 40 years. It didn't take much to get her talking. She told them that at one time their RV campground was three times the size it is now. The Mexican restaurant across the road, which was now closed, was the hottest place to go, before the town started dying.

She continued with her story, "First the railroad came, with their steam-powered trains; they needed coal to climb the steep Raton Pass into Colorado, which Raton had. Later Kaiser Steel used the Raton Basin's coal for its massive steel works. As the mines expanded, they took a heavy toll: The Dawson mine suffered two massive explosions a decade apart, in 1913 and 1923. Crosses marking the graves of more than 380 miners who died in the two accidents line the local cemetery." She said she lost two Uncles in the second accident.

Because of all the money, "Horseracing became major pastime for Raton locals beginning in 1946, and also brought in Texas oil barons and tourists from around the mid-West. Like coal, racing was in Raton's blood. But horseracing died out 1992 when the La Mesa track near town closed."

She said, "By 1950 the coal mines started closing one by one, beginning with Dawson. The nail that finally killed the town was when the last mine closed, which was the York Canyon, in 2003. Media mogul Ted Turner bought the Vermejo Park ranch that included the York Canyon Mine with no plans to reopen it."

As they were walking back to the RV, Frank told Aggie well that explains a lot about the big old empty houses we saw yesterday. She had to agree with him.

The snow was gone by noon, according to the weather woman; it was going to be in the 60's for the next couple of days. The storm hit Denver, CO, pretty hard, a lot harder than it did in Raton. They were glad they were going east, back to Texas. After it warmed up a little, they took the girls out for a walk around the campground. By the looks of it, the campground must have been huge at one time, everything was in disarray now. But you could tell it used to be quite the place. The dogs were having a great time, they were glad to be out of the RV. The rest of the day was just hanging out around the RV and getting ready to head to Amarillo, TX. They just planned on spending one night there, and then heading on to Whitney Lake, Thousand Trails. They found their next camp site in the Passport catalog; it's supposed to be on the east side of Amarillo, called KOA Camper Park. Passport has up to 50% discount on many campgrounds. This is the third site they have used from the catalog, so far it's worked out.

CHAPTER 9

Welcome back to Texas!

After driving for about four hours it was time to turn off the highway to the next campsite, according to the directions they had found in the Passport catalog. The RV Park should have been about a mile down the side road from the highway. As they drove down the road they saw an RV campground on the right-hand side but as they got closer, it looked like it was abandoned, or a trailer park. No cars, just a few parked RVs around the outer edge.

Aggie was in the lead, she radioed to Frank that this is supposed to be the place where we are suppose to camp tonight. But I don't see any name on the campground, let's go a little farther down the road and see if we can find another place. As Aggie headed down the road in front of Frank, she wanted to put some distance between them, so if she did see it she could give him enough time to slow down and pull into the new campground.

They drove another 2 miles but there was nothing out there except fields. Aggie radioed to Frank and let him know that he needs to turn right. We'll go around the block, Aggie told him. Granted the block was 2 miles by 2 miles long. They ended up back at the highway where they originally came in on. She radioed Frank again and suggested that they go check out the first campground they originally saw. Frank radioed back and agreed with her it can't hurt, he told her!

Aggie pulled in first and discovered it was the right place; she saw the sign, it was inside the gate. She radioed Frank and told him to come on in. As they pulled in an older gentlemen came out and welcomed them. He told Frank just park wherever there is an opening. Frank told him thanks and waited for Aggie to go find a place, as he followed behind her. It wasn't a big place, maybe 40 spaces. It looked like someone's field that they made into a RV campground.

They drove around the grounds; there wasn't much to choose from. The ones that were open had big muddy ruts in the middle of the parking space, because of the last rain storm. Other spaces looked like the electricity wasn't working in them; they had a bag on the power pole. Frank radioed Aggie, and told her let's keep going down the road and find something else. Aggie radioed back, Roger that!

As they started to pull out of the campground the older gentleman waved Frank down. He told Frank that there were other parking spaces over there, as he pointed in the direction of a grassy area; we had not gone too before. As Aggie was watching them, wondering what was going on. He told Frank to follow him. Frank radioed Aggie and told her what he said, there's another spot we had not seen. Aggie thought to herself I guess we are staying here tonight. Frank followed him; he led them to a nice little spot. He got out of his truck and pointed to Frank where to park the RV. The guy asked if this would be ok, and Frank told him it would be fine. He told Frank, he could pay at the building over there. He pointed to a little building by the gate. He explained to Frank, that there are envelopes, and a drop box to put the money in. Frank shook his hand and said thanks. The older gentleman got into his truck and drove away. Agatha got out of the car, and told Frank not bad.

There was a house on one side, which looked empty, and a trailer on the other side with a fence around. It sounded like there were a few dogs in it; they could hear the dogs barking. Aggie told Frank it sounds like they have a few dogs in there. Frank had to agree with her, they were making a lot of racket.

There wasn't much to setting up camp; they were only going to be there one night. It was a nice evening, no rain, or wind for a change. They decided to walk around the campground. As they walked around, they spotted a few donkeys and some cattle in a nearby pen; there wasn't much else to see.

Around 6 PM the neighbor, the one with the fenced yard, came home. It was just one guy living there, as far as Aggie could tell. He went into the trailer, within seconds it sounded like a dog pound. Aggie watched out the side window to see what happened next. The guy opened the trailer door and out came a good 20 dogs of all ages. It looked like a Chihuahua farm. Aggie called to Frank, who was in the bedroom, "Check out the dog pound next door!" Frank came out of the bedroom, and said, "Man that's a lot of dogs, I bet it stinks in there!" Aggie replied back, you thought two dogs were a lot.

It was fun to watch the dogs; she could tell they were really happy to be outside. Pretty soon the neighbor called the dogs back into the trailer; a few of them didn't look like they wanted to go back in. He called them again, and they went running back into the trailer. The rest of the evening was quite. They took the girls out for a short walk and called it a night. Next stop somewhere past Wichita Falls, TX.

The next morning the neighbor let his dogs out around 7 a.m., they barked a few times, then went and did their business. The girls watched with Aggie as their owner came to the door and called them back in. There may be a lot of them, but they are well behaved. Frank went out and disconnected everything, and Aggie put things up and they were on their way in 20 minutes.

After driving for three hours, Frank was getting a little tired, so they decided to stop at the next RV campground. Aggie took the lead so she could give Frank a heads up when she saw one. She spotted one about twenty miles down the road, as she went under an over pass, it was on the right. She radioed Frank there was one on the right, he radioed back looks good let's turn around and stay there for the night.

The next exit was Iowa Park, TX, they went over the over pass, another 2 mile U-turn. As they were coming to the RV Park, there were two police cars, which had a car pulled over with four teenagers in it; they had them against their car. Once inside the campground there were about six rigs, all looked like they were permanent. They pulled up to the building in the center of the Park; it was another self service camp ground. It was a nice little parking area; it was called B & S RV Park. They didn't have any cash, so Aggie wrote a check. She told Frank we really need to carry cash with us, he agreed with her. About that time the police let the kids go. After they got settled in, Aggie made dinner. After dinner Frank went to bed to watch TV, he just didn't feel well.

The next morning he was still tired, so they decided to spend one more day there. Their reservation at Lake Whitney wasn't for another day anyway. The park had a fence around it, which was a good thing. That evening there were cattle everywhere, if not for the fence they could have had visitors. Which normally wouldn't be a problem, but they were all long horns, and they didn't what the dogs chasing them. It was a slow day, but that evening they drove over to Iowa City, to see what was there. It was a small town; most of the businesses were along the freeway.

After they returned to the rig, they took the girls for a little walk; there really wasn't much area to walk them. That evening a few of the locals came home, it looked like they worked in the oil fields. They were dirty from top to bottom. They called it a night early, Frank was feeling better, and it was going to be a four to five hour drive tomorrow.

CHAPTER 10

Lake Whitney, TX

They arrived at Lake Whitney Thousand Trails around two; they found a nice spot to the front of the park. It was a nice private area; there were small cedar trees all around. They found a nice space that had shade for most of the day and sun in late afternoons. There wasn't anyone parked close to them, but the weekend was coming, which normally meant the campground would fill up.

There were of course, the full timers, but they were on the other side. The nice thing was that there were lots of places to walk. According to the campground map there were all kinds of hiking trails on the property.

For the next couple of days they walked around the campground, it was five miles from one end to the other. They knew this because they had walked it a couple of times. They were walking the dogs down by the lake one morning, when they heard what sounded like a pack of dogs barking, and the sound was getting closer.

As they got closer, Frank raised his walking stick above his head and started yelling at them, trying to scare them away. But they continued to come toward them. Aggie told him to use his command voice, so he did. He started yelling again, this time in his command voice. No one messed with Frank when his used it, not even Aggie. It's hard to explain, it's much deeper and stronger than his normal voice. I guess the best way to explain it is when your father scolds you. The dogs stopped barking, by this time Aggie had both their dogs in her arms. Then there was no more barking, they could hear the dogs running away. Aggie told Frank it's that command voice, it'll scare anything.

Aggie waited for a couple more minutes before putting the dogs back on the ground. They continued to walk down to the lake, it was a beautiful blue, but there was no Beach area, with 5 foot cliffs around the lake on their side. They walked along the lake side for a little while and then headed back to their rig.

It was nice not having to plan on moving to the next place for a while. The plan was to stay at Lake Whitney for three weeks before they moved again.

Aggie has a Texas map that she uses to keep track of every road they go on, she highlights them in orange. Her Texas map looked like it has varicose veins. She has done this with each of the states they have been in. She also had different colored pens for each year that they are on the road.

Aggie was looking at her map and discovered there were two large state parks not far from the Lake Whitney campground. It was time to go exploring! They made a picnic lunch and loaded up the dogs and headed out to the State Park campgrounds.

The first State Park they went to required them to pay and they decided they didn't want to see it that bad, so they went to the next one. They explained to the Ranger they just wanted to check out the campground. The Ranger told them no problem and let them in with a temporary pass. The campground was huge and right on the lake. As they were going out of the park, a big Bob Cat ran across in front of them. Aggie told Frank, I'm glad were in the Jeep, instead of walking the dogs. It was huge, and didn't seem to care they were there. After it got to the other side, it turned then looked at them, and slowly walked into the woods.

It normally doesn't take any longer to go in a circle, than going back the way you came. It's a good way to see more country and little towns. On the way home they saw a few more road runners, and a herd of long horns.

The lake was beautiful; they saw a nice little park on the lake. They decided to stop and let the girls out for a little bit. They didn't have to tell the dogs to get out. Aggie barely opened the door, and Susi jumped out, followed by Sage. Aggie didn't get a chance to put the leashes on the dogs before Sage took off after a rabbit.

Aggie yelled at her to come back, but she was determined to catch that rabbit. But the rabbit was too smart for her; she had gone inside the cactus bushes. Sage ran in after it, and got as far as sticking her head inside the cactus bush, she was determined to follow the rabbit into the bush, but she pulled out immediately. She yelped when she started to back out, and stopped. By then Aggie had caught up to her and helped her get out of the cactus bushes, she picked her up. Aggie looked into the hole where the rabbit had gone and she could see the little thing looking back at her. Aggie guessed that the rabbit was pretty confident the dog wouldn't follow her in there. Aggie looked at Sages face and found a couple of needles sticking out of her nose. She pulled the stickers out of her face, Sage didn't like it one little bit. She checked the rest of Sages body and she was fine. She scolded her about running off, but Sages really didn't care. She was still looking at where the rabbit had disappeared. Aggie could see it in Sage face; it looked like she was thinking which way did it go? As she moved her head side to side at the hole.

Aggie hooked the dog leash up to her and put her down. Sage wasn't going to go willingly, so Aggie started dragging her back to the picnic table. Sage was still determined to get that rabbit. Aggie told Sage she was a bad girl, but Sage really couldn't understand why. All she wanted to do is play with the rabbit.

They sat at the picnic table and watched the boats on the lake and enjoy their lunch. There were all types of boats on the lake, kind of like RV's, there is too many to list. She tried to make a list of all the RVs that they had seen, and it didn't work out. There are just too many different types and models around.

They noticed a large house across the lake that looked like a castle, it was huge. Frank dug out the binoculars to check it out; he told Aggie there is a naked lady on the deck! Aggie responded with your lying! Frank turned to her and smiled, maybe! Aggie took the binoculars away from him as he laughed; she told him there no naked lady there, as she hit him on the arm and laughed. It looks like it might be a restaurant, but she really couldn't tell. They decided to go check it out; they loaded up the dogs and the picnic basket and headed in the direction of where they thought the road might be. But they couldn't find the road that would lead them to it, after a while they gave up and headed home.

Aggie had put a roast in the slow cooker before they left and she figured it would be about ready by the time they got home. She loved using her slow cooker on days like this; all she had to do is take food out of the slow cooker and put it on their plates.

When they opened the door they could smell the roast, 10 minutes later they were sitting at the table eating their dinner. Of course they had to feed the dogs before they could eat, and the dogs demanded their fair share. Otherwise, they would just beg for their food. Again Aggie really loves her slow cooker.

The next two days they just walked around the campground enjoying just sitting around doing nothing. But as usual, after a few days Aggie started getting restless and wanted to go for a ride. They decided to go east this time and see what was out there. Aggie saw a sign that said Hillsboro, she turned to Frank and said doesn't Larie and Dean live in Hillsboro, Oregon? Frank responded yes that's where they have their house. They decided to follow the signs to Hillsboro, Texas and check out the town. They went down FM 22, and saw another sign saying Hillsboro, so they turned right and there was another sign so they turned left. After driving around for 30 minutes, Frank asked Aggie, "Wasn't Hillsboro supposed to be a nice size town?" All I've seen so far is fields, and a couple of little towns. They went another 10 miles and there was still nothing, and no more signs saying Hillsboro. They saw a sign saying Whitney, somehow or another they ended up on a back road going back to Whitney. By some means they lost Hillsboro, so they headed back home.

Aggie checked out her Texas map later on that evening, and also went online to find out exactly where Hillsboro was. She was determined that she was going to find it. She told Frank yeah it's on the map, but some of the roads that we were on today are not on the map.

Weird! Frank told her, well I guess we will have to try again. Aggie reminded Frank they had to go to Waco tomorrow, to go to the VA hospital for his blood test. It's only 40 miles away, she showed him on the map where it was at and said that they could do a big circle and come back by the way of Hillsboro. It's supposed to be right off of the freeway.

Frank told her it sounds like a plan, is there anything interesting in Hillsboro to see? Aggie went online and started reading what the Hillsboro web site had.

Well Hillsboro was named for Hill County. According to the web site, "Bonnie and Clyde's took the Peterson family hostage at their own farm. Later the Petersons said that Bonnie and Clyde held them at gun point until they surrendered their barn for them to sleep in for a few nights before running again." Well at least they didn't kill them, Frank told Aggie, Aggie responded, True!

She continued to read "Hillsboro is known for its abundance of restored Victorian homes and its historic county courthouse, which on January 1, 1993 was heavily damaged by an electrical fire. It was rebuilt, courtesy of donations from around the world and two concerts sponsored by Hill County native Willie Nelson. Restoration of the building which was built in 1890, it took over six years and $9 million dollars to complete. The courthouse won the Downtown Association's 1999 award for "Best Restoration". The Hill County courthouse is eight miles from Willie Nelson's hometown, Abbott." Maybe we can go check out Abbott sometime, Aggie said.

There was also a movie made there, called the Bottle Rocket. I don't think we ever saw it, have we? Aggie asked Frank. I don't think so was his reply. Aggie read, "They used the Days Inn motel, the Hillsboro High School football stadium, and Highway 171 leading out of Hillsboro for the movie." See there are some things to see; the courthouse looks pretty cool, as she showed Frank the pictures she found on the website.

Sounds like a full day, Frank told Aggie. The next morning they were up and out the door by 8:00 a.m., the dogs had been walked and had food and water for the day. Aggie had mapped out the directions to Waco, and it was going to be mostly back roads.

The drive started out nice and easy, but as they got closer to Waco the traffic became a nightmare, after a few U-turns, they found the VA Clinic, it was huge. It was an army post, many years ago. They wandered around for awhile and then decided to take the freeway back and go through Hillsboro. They saw a sign said 20 miles to Hillsboro, then one for 10, and then there was nothing. They missed Hillsboro again. Aggie turned to Frank, What the Hell, how can we miss a whole town. Frank responded, I have no clue, its like were in the twilight zone. They followed the signs back to Whitney, and ended back at the campground around 4:00 p.m. Aggie told Frank, Tomorrow we're going to Hillsboro, and we are not stopping until we find it! Frank laughs and agreed with her.

Aggie went on line, and looked at her maps, she couldn't understand how they could miss the town, but tomorrow they will find it, she assured Frank. Frank smiled and said, "We will see!"

According to the map, they just needed to get on road 22; it should run right into town. It's just 24 miles away. As they drove through Whitney and headed down 22, they saw their first mistake, they should have stayed on 22, after about 20 minutes, they drove into downtown Hillsboro, and to the left was the courthouse. Aggie turned to Frank, well that was easy, as she smiled at him. He just laughed and shook his head, and said your right! Well let's go check out the 9 million dollar courthouse.

The courthouse looked like a castle; it was all white, with large pillar in front of the entrance ways. There were at least 40 arched windows, in the front, some were strain glass windows. It's beautiful! Aggie told Frank, as they walked into the front door, he had to agree with her. They walked into the large hallway, and on each side there were large maple doors. Frank asked Aggie; why do these courthouses have 15 ft. doors in them. Aggie smiled and said; maybe they knew something we don't know. The floor was yellow and brown, it was interesting, there was an iron staircase going up to the second and third floor. They went down to the basement, it was so quiet, and it looked like it may be their break area. The walls were decorated cement blocks, and the doors were all iron rod, maybe it was the jail house at one time.

Then they went back upstairs and talked to the police officer that was on duty. He told them about the great fire and how the bell in the tower fell all the way to the basement floor. He was an interesting fellow, and had a lot of stories to tell about his town. After talking to him they decided to walk around town and see the historical buildings in the downtown area. It's always interesting to see the little towns that have been forgotten. Aggie took a few more pictures of the courthouse and was heading home, when they saw historical Tavern. They just looked at each other, and pulled over to check it out. But it was closed, Frank told Aggie maybe next time. Yea, it's a little early to have a drink anyway, Aggie replied, but it is 5 o'clock somewhere. They got back in their Jeep and headed home.

The next week went by fast, Lake Whitney campground was nice and the Rangers and Manager were great. They had something going on all the time. Aggie and Frank did go to Paris and Athens,

TX on one of their drives, there wasn't much there, they did stop at the Paris cemetery, it was an older one. But it looked like it had been vandalized; many of the head stones had been broken in half. Aggie couldn't understand why anyone would do something like that. Athens was a bigger town, but it looked like it was having a hard time too. Most of the businesses were closed down.

After a couple of days staying home, Aggie was ready to go explode again. Frank suggested going to Glen Rose, TX. He had an Uncle named that. He told her it is also supposed to have dinosaur foot prints, which is all it took for Aggie to agree. Aggie went online, and found out it was only 35 miles from them and it also had a Wildlife Reserve, and a place called Dinosaur world.

Aggie also found this online about Glen Rose, TX. "The area was first settled in 1849 by Charles Barnard, who opened a trading post near Comanche Peak. After the region became a federal Indian reservation in 1855, Barnard moved his business to Fort Belknap. In 1859 when the reservation was abolished, he returned to the area and built the first store on what is now the site of Glen Rose."

"A three-story stone gristmill, (grinds grain into flour) was constructed along the Paluxy River and the town that grew up around it became known as Barnard's Mill. The mill was sold to T.C. Jordan of Dallas in 1871 for $65,000. Jordan's wife, a native of Scotland, decided to rename the town Rose

Glen to reflect the area's natural surroundings. The citizens later voted to call the community **Glen Rose**. Throughout the period from the 1900s to the 1920s, Glen Rose was home to approximately 1,000 people."

"During Prohibition, the area was a center of moonshining. Glen Rose city became known as the "whiskey woods" capital of the state. During the post-war years, the population of Somervell County declined from 3,071 in 1940 to 2,542 in 1950 as many residents moved in search of greater employment opportunities. At the same time, Glen Rose grew from 1,050 residents in 1940 to 1,248 in 1950. The construction of the Comanche Peak Nuclear Power Plant in the mid-1970s brought financial advantages and new residents to the Glen Rose area. The city experienced a 34 percent increase in population between 1970 and 1980. The nuclear plant came to dominate the local economy."

They left camp around 10 that morning to go to Glen Rose; they parked in the middle of town, by the museum and the old courthouse. They were both closed; they are only open on the weekend. The first thing they noticed was the siding of the buildings. They were unusual, as they were made out of petrified wood and old pieces of logs. There were also large agate stones imbedded between some of the wood. In the middle of the town square, there was a Texas star which served as a fountain and the walls of the fountain was made with the logs. They looked like petrified logs, going every which way and then a trick sealer painted over them. Aggie suggested to Frank, they could do something like that on the outside of the house with their rocks and petrified wood. He just smiled, and continued to walk along. As they walked around downtown they saw more log walls on houses and business buildings. Some even had large Agates incorporated with the logs. They were unique walls, neither one had ever seen these types of walls before. The town had a lot of different antique and tourist shops.

They wandered to the back roads of the town, where they found more old houses, and more distinctive designs of rocks and logs. But it was time to head to the wildlife reserve, they had found on the Internet.

The wildlife reserve was called "Fossil Rim Wildlife Centers Scenic Wildlife Drive", what a mouthful. According to the brochure it is an 1800 acres reserve and there is over 1100 animals roaming freely in the large pastures. You had an option to either take the tour bus or take your own car; they decided to take their car. The cashier told them that it should take about two hours to go on the 9 ½ miles drive. There is a little rest stop overlook with tourist things to do, halfway through the tour. Well she didn't say it that way but that's what she meant! They also offered food bags for the animal. Aggie and Frank decided to pass on them. It was a small bag of corn mix, for $7.

The flyer that they received had pictures of all the animals that were on the reserve, by Aggies count there was 27 different types of animal. They were first greeted by American Bison. It was nice to see them, Aggie told Frank, after not seeing any of them at the "Land between the Lakes" reserve in Kentucky.

There were Addax, the first one had two long horns, the second Addax had one missing horn, and it kind of looked like a unicorn. Addax looks like a mix of deer and goat, with curve horns. Every time they stopped the car, the animals would start coming towards them, and one wild turkey actually started running at them. Frank told Aggie I guess we should have purchased the corn! Aggie had to agree with him, it might have been a better idea.

It was fun to watch the other cars with kids in them; the kids would throw one piece at a time at the animals. The animals were very patient, and waited for the next piece to be thrown. After passing three or four cars they got to the view point. There was quite a variety of animals to see, it was a cool day so most were out wandering about.

After the midpoint, they saw Giraffe and Elk eating together, and then they went to the Cheetah viewing enclosure. The lady at the office told them that they have had over 190 Cheetah born here. They started raising them in 1984, there is no place else that have had so many new born.

As they were leaving Aggie told Frank it's nice seeing live animals instead of the stuffed ones that they saw in the museums. Frank had to agree, and said let's go see the Dinosaurs! She smiled at him, sounds good to me. The place they were talking about is called, "Dinosaur World" it has over 100 life size Dinosaurs, and a museum with fossils, and minerals. It is the "largest attraction dedicated to giants of years past!" It is on 20 acres, as you walk along the path, with each turn there was a new dinosaur, larger then life. It was pretty cool; there was a Fossil dig, Bone yard, and a large play ground for kids. Frank told Aggie, this would be a great place to take the younger grandkids. Aggie responded back the big kids too!

When they entered the building Aggie noticed right away that they had minerals and fossils for sell too. Aggie couldn't help herself she had to check out the minerals first before going into the Dinosaur world.

It was a fascinating place to see. But the ones that really got their attention was the one that had a family unit, there was one of Apatosaurus with their necks sticking high about the trees. What a wild site to see, it was cool the way they showed the different dinosaur in a herd environment, with their little babies. At the end they had the famous Tyrannosaurs' standing there ready to eat you.

Most of the things were set up for kids to do things; it was hard for Aggie to not do them. Where are the grandkids when you need them? She thought to herself. The museum was wonderful; there were displays of animated dinosaurs, in their environment. They would move around and make different growling sounds.

Aggie couldn't help herself; she had found a very large mineral rock in the store before they went out to the park. It was from Brazil stone and it was calling to her. It has been a while since they had purchased anything for their home museum. When the cashier picked up the stone, she acted surprise how heavy it was, it must weigh at least 75 pounds. It was as large as a basketball; they weren't sure where they were going to store it in the RV. But she'll figure it out.

The weekends were always filled with things to do around the campground. This weekend they went to a dance at the lodge, and a flag ceremony for Memorial Day, and Aggie had a book signing for one of her travel books. But it was time to go, next stop Bay Landing outside of Bridgeport, it was only 114 miles away from Lake Whitney. It looked like a straight shot to the next site according to the map.

Here's a little history about Bridgeport, TX, it has ten Historical Markers: "World War II training site, Republic of Texas Santé Fe Expedition in Wise County, Toll Bridge & Old Bridgeport, Bridgeport Coal Mines, Bridgeport Lodge No. 587, Col. William H. Hunt, and Republic of Texas Santa Fe Expedition in Wise County". There are three Historical markers for the first United Methodist,

Presbyterian, and the Baptist Church". Except for the Church, they only reason you would know these things happened here, is because of the markers.

"Coal was once a staple of Bridgeport's economy. Coal had been discovered in Bridgeport in the later part of the 19th century. Diggers hit a vein 60 feet deep while seeking water. Mine No. 1 lies under Northeast Bridgeport, and entire area is honeycombed with tunnels and shafts. It had 500 employees at the high point of the mines. Most of the mines closed in 1929 due to increased use of oil and gas. The last mine closed in the early 1940's."

Aggie had been reading this to Frank, and suggested maybe they could go find one of these mines. I would like to get some coal for our correction. Frank replied yeah that would be neat.

CHAPTER 11

Welcome to Bay Landing, Bridgeport

They arrived at the campground around noon; they found a great place across from the lodge. It had a nice shaped tree, and a nice size space. The other side didn't have septic, so they fell lucky to get this spot; the person had just left that morning.

They set up camp and walked around the campground checking out the lodge and the surrounding area. When they got back to the RV, there was a Ranger at the trailer next to them. Then he came over to them and told them the power was off. The Ranger told them, they had no clue how long the power would be off; the electric company cut the main line.

The fact that it was in the 90's and would be for the rest of the week, really added to the problem. The rest of the camp sites were filled, because of the holiday. The Ranger offered everyone in their section a cabin to stay in for the night. There were 15 RV's set up in the section, which they called "Hollywood", where the power was out. The rest of the camp ground was affected too, but they set up generators to the lodge, pool and the other sections that were on the other side of the grounds. Frank guessed they must have run out of generators.

Aggie told the Ranger they had two dogs, and asked if that would be a problem, he told them No. They packed an overnight bag and headed over to the cabin. It seemed kind of odd that the row of cabins had power, while the rest of the campground had no power.

As they went into the cabin Frank told Aggie, not bad as they walked into the cabin. At least it doesn't move when we walk, he smiled at her. The air condition feels pretty good too, Aggie told Frank. The girls started checking out the place at once, first on the bed, and then the couch. Aggie said it looks like the girls approve of it. That evening they took the girls for another walk and checked out the lake. The cabin was in a nice area, it had a view of the lake, and screen room on the back of it.

The next morning they found a Ranger to find out what was going on, he told them it looks like the power won't be on for awhile. They went over to Penelope and hung out for awhile and then went back to the cabin. On their fourth day; they decided it was time to move back into Penelope. So they moved over to the other side of the campground. The cabin was nice, but it was one big room with just one TV.

By now the holiday weekend was over and most of the campers had already left. It was pretty easy to find a space; the only problem there was no septic. Which wasn't a big deal, they were only going to be there for two more weeks, and they had honey bucket service. Honey bucket service is when someone comes around with a tank trailer and empties your black and grey water.

They found a place, where they could back up to the lake, with an open field in front of them. Normally, it would be filled with RVs. It had a large tree and both the spaces on each side were open. They felt like they had the place to themselves, quite a difference from the weekend before.

Aggie told Frank, if I had to give anyone advise about going full time, I would tell them to make sure you have a separate bedroom. I don't care how much you love someone; everyone needs a break from each other, and a place to do their own thing. Frank agreed, and told her, "Yeah, and even more so in the winter. Could you imagine being in a small RV, with all the bad weather, that we have been in." He laughed and told Aggie, "You wouldn't even get to watch your shows or do your writing." She laughs and said, I think it would be you missing your programs.

With the weather getting in the 90s by 10 a.m., they started getting out by 7. There was a nice hiking trail around the campground; they had built up to 10000 steps a day, which is nearly 5 miles a day. The first day at their new site, they started their walking. They didn't even get 1000 steps in when Frank started feeling weird and got chest pains. They turned around and went home, they figured it was because he hadn't taken his pills, and was dehydrated. After sitting and drinking water he felt better. He felt fine the rest of the day.

The next morning they went for their morning walk with the dogs. Agatha made sure that Frank had drunk a bottle of water before they headed out. She wanted to make sure he didn't get dehydrated again. But the weather was already in the 80s, and he started getting chest pain, after about 500 steps. Aggie asked Frank, do we need to go to the hospital? He told her No, I just didn't sleep well last night. Again they went home, and after a little bit Frank felt better. They just hung out around the RV; Frank went to bed and slept for a few hours. That evening he was fine, they took the dogs out for a little walk and he was fine.

The next morning they started out to walk the dogs, and didn't get 50 feet before his chest started hurting. Aggie told him enough is enough you're going to the hospital. They got back to the RV, and she looked on the internet for the closes emergency room. Frank told her, I'm fine, it's not hurting anymore. Aggie responded I don't care your going in! Frank didn't like the idea, but he knew Aggie wasn't going to take no for an answer. Aggie found the closet hospital it was in Decatur, TX, about 20 miles away. She asked Frank how he was feeling; did she need to call for ambulance? No, it doesn't hurt anymore, Frank told her. Aggie told him we're still going, get in the car. Just like a kid, never wants to do what is good for him.

They arrived at the hospital, and went into the emergency room, once they found out that he had chest pain, they didn't waste any time. They bought out a wheelchair, and rolled him off into the back. After taking blood test, chest x-ray and a few other tests, which took a few hours, they wanted to keep him over night. They wanted to do an angiogram in the morning. They agreed and they said it would be a few minutes. It had been four hours since they arrived at the hospital. Aggie asked the doctor what angiogram entails.

The doctor told them, "During an angiogram, a thin tube called a catheter is placed into a blood vessel in the groin (femoral artery or vein). The catheter is guided to the area to be studied. Then an iodine dye is injected into the vessel to make the area show clearly on the X-ray pictures. This method is known as conventional or catheter angiogram. The angiogram pictures can be made into regular X-ray films or stored as digital pictures in a computer."

"An angiogram can find a bulge in a blood vessel (aneurysm). It can also show narrowing or a blockage in a blood vessel that affects blood flow. An angiogram can show if coronary artery disease is present and how bad it is." We want to do it first thing in the morning the doctor continued, he looked at Frank, as if asking him if he agreed to it. Frank agreed, after asking a few more questions. The Dr. said great, we'll see you in the morning. As soon as they have a room they will take you up to the 5th floor.

Aggie told Frank she was going home, and would be back in the morning. It was hard to leave Frank there, but there wasn't much she could do, and the dogs needed to be walked back at the campground. Once she got home she called Frank to see how he was doing. He told her, "I'm fine, my chest pain is gone, and it seems silly for me to be here." They're going to do the test at 8, and it's going to take a couple of hours, so there no point in you coming in early.

It was a long night, waiting for morning to come for both of them. It's been a long time since they been apart. As Aggie was getting ready to head over to the hospital, Frank called and asked when she was coming in. She told him that she was on her way, what's up? Frank said the doctor wants to talk to us. What's wrong? She asked Frank. He told her you'll find out when you get here. She told him just tell me, he told her they want to do a triple bypass surgery.

Aggie didn't know what to say, all she could say is I'm on my way. Frank told her to go to the third floor, take a right out of the elevator. He told her, just let them know your there and the doctor will come out and talk to you. She told him Ok, I love you, and I'll see you soon.

It was the longest twenty miles; Aggie went to the third floor and told the receptionist who she was. After about fifteen minutes, they called her name. She held her breath, as she went through the door. The doctor met her on the other side of the door. He introduced himself, and told her what was going on. They didn't even finish the angiogram, they discovered that three of his arteries were almost closed, one was 97% and the other two are 95% closed. He needs a triple bypass surgery, he needs it right away, but he said he wanted to go back home to have it done. Aggie told the doctor no he needs to have it done here. I don't want him driving home and having heart attack. The doctor seemed relieved and agreed with her. He told her where she could find Frank; he's on this floor on the other end. Just push the button, tell the receptionist who you are, and they will let you in. Aggie thanked the doctor, and headed over to see Frank.

Frank seemed to be a little out of it, but was fine. He asked if she had talked to the doctor, and she told him yes. She told him about his arteries, and their doing the surgery tomorrow, first thing. He smiled and said, yea the doctor tapped me on my should during my procedure, and told me your getting a triple bypass surgery.

Aggie told him that I guess we better call the kids and the folks and let them know what's going on. Frank really didn't want to but he knew better. Of course, the kids all wanted to come here, but they told them to wait until later. You won't make it here before he goes in and he'll be out of it for a couple days. They agreed, and told Aggie to call them when he got out of surgery. They agreed, Aggie would call Maria, and she would call everyone else.

Another long day, Aggie headed home around 7 pm, and Frank was told they would be back at 4 am, to get him ready for surgery. At 4 am the nurses were there, they told Frank he needed to cut his beard off, and they shaved the hair off his chest, arms and legs. He had to take three sterol showers. At 6 a.m. they rolled him off to surgery, the nurse told that she would hold his hand until he fell asleep. As he waited for the anesthesia to work he notices Kathy's mask was moving as she said a little prayer for him. His last thought that Frank would recall later was how comforting that seemed.

It was going to be a 4 to 5 hours surgery, so Aggie waited until 10 am before heading in. She really didn't like hospitals, the less time she spends there the better she liked it. When she arrived they had just brought him in and were setting him up to stay for a few days. He still had tape on his eyes. Aggie asked the nurse why is there tape on his eyes? The nurse replied it can come off; she walked over and pulled it off. She told Aggie, he woke up once, but we put him back to sleep. A couple minutes later Frank woke up again, Aggie was holding his hand, he tried to pull the tube out of his mouth, but she stopped him. She could read it in his eyes; he wanted that air tube out! She asked the nurse how much longer the tube was going to be in, he wants it out. She told her he has to be awake for 30 minutes. She told Frank, but she could tell he didn't care, he wanted it out. So she held his hand, so he couldn't pull out the tube.

It was the longest 30 minutes, but the tube finally came out. First thing Frank said was, "I couldn't breathe!" The nurse told them, it's ok, she understood, but it's better to have it in, just in case something happens.

For the next couple hours, the nurse would remove tubes out of different parts of his body and then removed the machine that was connected to it. Every time Frank had pain, they would give him more morphine, and it would knock him out. They told them he would be there for at least a week. Frank got better and better, he was determined to get out of that hospital. On the third day he passed his last test, but the doctor wanted him to stay one more day. The fourth day came, and they told him he could go to the Rehab Center. He didn't want to go there, for physical therapy, but Aggie was set on having him go. He would get better care than she could give him in the RV. At the rehab center the nurse told them, "Normally, people are here for four weeks or more!" Frank wasn't going to stay any longer then he had to. If it wasn't for Aggie, he would have left the third day.

That weekend the kids came to see him, what an affair. They stayed for a few hours. They went out to the courtyard and laughed and talked about everything. Frank and Aggie enjoyed having the kids there, but it really wore them out. For the next two weeks, every time Aggie came in Frank was doing better; he was starting to eat a little more. So far he had lost 20 lbs. The nurse had told them that food just won't look good for awhile, and your taste may change. He was considered a falling risk, so they put alarm on his bed and wheelchair, so if he got up they would know. For Frank to leave the center, he had to pass more physical tests. He had to get out of bed, shower and walk by himself. Everyday Aggie would come in and visit for awhile, then go home walk the dogs, and mess around the RV.

One day she decided she wanted to stay home, she told Frank she would be in the next day. Then that evening she got the call, it was Frank they were going to take him to the emergency room. Something had popped in his chest, and he was in a lot of pain. He told Aggie, I didn't know if I should have called you. She replied, back of course you should, and I'm on my way. All the way in it hit her, she could lose her husband, as the tears started to come down her face, she told herself, and he'll be fine. She told herself; get yourself together old women, all you need to do is get in a car accident. Wouldn't that be a fine mess! They wouldn't have a clue, about where you lived, or your husband in the hospital, and what about the girls.

She arrived at the hospital, tears all gone, and ready to face whatever happens next. They told her where Frank was and she went to be with him. She could tell he was in so much pain, the first thing that came out of his mouth, "I'm sorry, I shouldn't have called you. Aggie just smiled at him, and told him if you hadn't I would have killed you. Frank laughed and said Yeah, that's what I figured! Aggie gave him a kiss, and held his hand. The doctor came in and talked to them about the test. Everything looks fine, we what to do another blood test, in an hour just to make sure, then she left the room.

Frank was in such pain that Aggie went out to flag down a nurse. They finally gave Frank some morphine for the pain; Aggie kidded him, that's why you're here you just wanted another hit of morphine. Frank smiled and the morphine kicked in, about 30 minute later he was back. As they sat there and talked, all of sudden Aggie heard this loud pop coming out of Frank's chest, and Frank was in pain. Aggie got up and told Frank I'm going to go get the nurse, that didn't sound good at all! She found the nurse and told her what happened. She acted like it was no big deal, and she would let the doctor know.

When she got back to Frank, he wasn't in pain; he smiled and told her I think whatever popped earlier just popped back in.

It was the weirdest thing to hear this loud pop come out of someone's chest. When Frank had told her earlier about the pop, she thought it was something different; she wasn't sure what to think of it. Accept that it was nothing like she heard before.

The doctor came in a little while later and told them everything looks good, she couldn't explain the popping sounds. But his x-ray looked good, we'll send him back to the center, we have a driver that will take him. By now it was 9 pm, so Aggie told Frank she better get home, and she'll call him when she gets there. They kissed good-by, they put Frank in a wheelchair, and Aggie headed home. What a night, she hoped there wouldn't be any more like this. She called Frank to say good night, he told her he was feeling much better, and he was sorry he scared her again. She replied, no problem, you better call me if anything else happens. Love ya Good night!

For the next couple of weeks everything was going well, Aggie had rented their space for another month, and every day Frank got a little better. Then she got the call, it was Frank, "Guess what honey, I get to come home today. All I have to do is take a shower by myself and I'll be home free. What time can you pick me up? Now! Aggie replied. Frank told her, how about three. Aggie agreed I'll see you then. She arrived at two and talked to the nurse, and found out what she needed to know. Frank was never too good about asking questions. They packed him up and he said his good-byes, he was so happy to be leaving.

When they got home, the girls went crazy, they were all over him and wouldn't leave his side, and when he went to bed, they were there. There was no way he was going anywhere without them. Each day they would walk a little farther. One day they were out walking around the campground with the dogs. As always they watched out for dogs that were around the trailers. After being attacked three times, they were always on the lookout for loose dogs. Aggie saw a bull massive, but he was on a leash, so she just pulled the girls over to the other side of the road. About that time the bull massive came running at them, she started backing up more and pulling the dogs to her. All the while the bull massive had been pulling on his rope, barking at them. Suddenly the rope popped, and he came running at them. Susi took off running and went behind Frank. Sheba didn't know what was going on. Aggie was still backing up pulling their dogs with her, when all of sudden she fell backwards. As she was going down she saw Sheba underneath the bull massive, and that's all she wrote. Aggies hint the back of her head on a small rock. She couldn't move for a few minutes, then Frank reach down to help her up. She started to reach for him, and then remembered he wasn't suppose to lift anything over 10 lbs. She pulled her hand back and told him no. The owner of the attack dog was there by then. The wife had the dog back at their trailer and Sheba was alright. Aggie asked the husband to help her up; she told him Frank just had open heart surgery, he can't pick anything up over 10 lbs. He reaches down and helped her up, he told them he was so sorry, the rope was new, but he broke it.

Aggies's head was really hurting, so she didn't have much to say. As long as her girls were ok, she was good. They walked home, and Frank told her, I hit that dog with my cane when it started going back. Susi took off running and stayed behind me. Things happen so fast sometimes. Later that day the owner and his family came over to check on Aggie, and couldn't stop telling her how sorry they were. Aggies head hurt for a few days, but she was fine. It was better than what Frank had just been though.

After a week of hanging around the campground, Aggie was getting cabin fever. She went on line and looked at the maps, to see if there was anything of interest close to them. It was still hard for Frank to ride in the car, every hole or bump in the road, caused him a great deal of pain, but he tried not to show it, but Aggie could tell. She found a historical town just fifteen miles away that looked interesting, it was called Wizard Wells, TX.

It didn't take them long to get to Wizard Wells. They drove through town looking for the historical marker, but they didn't see anything. They turned the car around and went back through the town, hoping to spot it. When Frank spotted the marker, it was on Wizard St. It sat on a little hill, so they couldn't see it coming from the direction they came in.

To their surprise, it was an interesting place; the historical marker had a lot of information, it read: "The Kiowa Indians first visited this location and used the mineral waters for medicinal purposes. George Washington Vineyard settled here in the 1870's."

"Those seekng treatments often camped along Bean's creek in their wagons. Soon three hotels and several bath houses opened to serve the increased visitor population. The town of Vineyard was laid out in 1882 and J.H. Grisham opened the first general store The town later included several churches, a newspaper, school, sawmilll, blacksmith shop, and post office."

"In 1898 the Rock Island Railroad bypassed Vineyard and Sebbe community was started. Visitors arriving by train took a hack to the resort. H.F. Stamper and his sons, Clint and H.F. JR., petitioned the legislature in 1915 and the name of Vineyard became "Wizard Wells", Sebree was changed to Vineyard."

It is funny how much they can get on a little sign, Aggie told Frank. Everything that the marker wrote about was either closed down, the building was gone or being used for something else. The old hotel looked like it had seen better days, but the well was still there, but covered up. As they were looking around, Aggie saw a healing circle. It was about thirty-five feet across, it was divided in two sections you could walk around inside, like a labareth. They walked over to it and decide to walk it.

With Frank just having heart surgery, they figuered it couldn't hurt. A healing circle is a large circle, that has paths that go around inside the circle. This one had stones marking the paths, and a large stone in the middle and with crystals and small figrines to help with the healing. Aggie had seen a few different ones, this was the first permanent one. She had to take a couple of pictures of it. There were stones and minerals though out the circle. It looked like people were leaving gifts for the power of the circle. Whoever made it, took a lot of time to keep the area clean and positive energy there.

Frank hadn't used one before, so Aggie explained, try to clear your mind and ask to be healed. Enjoy the walk and let everything else go. Normally, you would use sage smoke to help clean your aura before you enter the circle. But we don't have any, so just take three deep breaths. It took about 30 minutes to walk around inside the circle. Aggie kept pointing out the different items inside the circle. They both could feel the energy from the healing power. As weird as it sounds, Aggie had a bad headache still from the fall, and her back was hurting. When she came out of the circle, both we're gone. Frank told her he felt better too.

They walked around a little more, it was kind of like a park. Frank found a wind chine hanging from a tree, it was almost as big as he was. There was all kinds of things to look at there, it had a lot of charm. Aggie enjoyed finding this type of places, but it was time to get Frank home.

The next couple of weeks was spent taking Frank to therpy three times a week. It was hard for Frank to ride in the car, everytime there was a bump in the road, it hurt him. After therpy they would go home so Frank could take a nap. It was hard for Aggie to see Frank like this, but it was better then him dying. The doctor had told them he was lucky he didn't have a heart attack, Frank's heart looked really good. According to the doctor by not having a heart attack, and just chest back, there was no damage to his heart.

When Frank was taking his naps, Aggie would do things around the house, or look out the window and watch the wild life. The animals were always up to something. Once a squirrel was gathering nuts and the birds would attack him trying to get the nuts it had gathered earlier. The squirrel knew if he climbed the tree, the bird couldn't get it. Once the bird flew away the squirrel would come out of the tree. Then he would hide under the trailer next to them and then make a run for the trees. One time a rabbit was making a run for it, when a bird flew down and attacked it. It was a cottontail rabbit, and the bird flew away with a mouth full of cottonball. The rabbit didn't slow down, so Aggie figuered it wasn't the first time. They have also saw a turkey, many deers, rats, rabbits, squirrels, shrews, and turtles while they have been there.

Frank was doing good, but still had a long way to go. It wasn't a very long drive to the next site at Texoma. They had been there earlier this year, after that they planned on heading east, though Arkansas to Tennessee, then who knows where. Bay Landing was nice, it was just to bad they didn't have more septic sites or at least a better shower/bath house. The laudary room wasn't that great either.

It was going on week seven, they had one more week, then they were planning on heading out next week. Frank was doing good in physical therpy, but he still needed to go to work outs, the center transfered his records to the Bridgeport physical therpy center. He'll be going there for another three weeks, three times a week. The week went by pretty fast, the morning of the move they were out by 10 a.m.. The weather was nice it looked like clear sailing.

As usual things are not what they seem, as they came onto I35, somehow they missed their turn, and ended up going into OK. They turned around and went back into Texas. Aggie took the lead and she saw where they should have turned off earlier, and radioed Frank to turn at the next exit. After that it was clear sailing, they arrived at their new site around two and set up camp.

There weren't many open sites to choose from, the campground was pretty full. The fact that they were forced to find a 50 amp site, that cut the choices of sites in half. But they did find a nice place to park; there were cabins and a hiking trail close by.

CHAPTER 12

Welcome back to Texoma, TX

rriving on a Friday is never a good thing; the place was pretty full with only a couple of weeks until school starting it looked like everyone was trying to enjoy the rest of summer. After the weekend it emptied out, but there was still some kids there that were being home schooled. It's surprising how many people live and work from their RV and home school their kids these days.

With Frank going to therapy three times a week, they would go for long walks on the days he didn't go. They had to go to Gainesville for the therapy, which was 25 miles away, and started at 10 a.m., so normally after therapy they would go for a ride and find a place to have lunch.

The people at the center were amazing; Frank was doing great according to the nurse, Kristi. Every time they went in there was always something going on. Aggie would visit with the staff or another wife waiting for her husband to get done. The therapy would take an hour, each time Frank would do more exercise each session.

Aggie was told about a town not far from the center; it looks like a German town and has German decedents. When they got home, Aggie looked up the history of the town. The next time they went to therapy they wanted to check it out.

This is what Aggie found out about the town: "It was found in 1887 by the Missouri-Kansas-Texas Railroad. The Railroad constructed a line from Gainesville to Henrietta that passed through the site that would become Muenster."

"The town was subsequently founded in 1889 by German Catholic settlers. Carl and Emil Flusche invited other German Catholics to join them. The town was originally to be called "Westphalia", but since the name Westphalia, Texas, was already taken, Muenster was selected instead in honor of Muenster, the capital of Westphalia, but these cities are not sister-cities. Many residents still spoke German in day-to-day life up until the First World War, after which the language was no longer taught in the schools and steadily declined in use. With more than 90% of the population German and Catholic, the city has preserved many German customs, and still produces traditional foods at the local meat market and bäckerei."

They were looking for a German restaurant, but they were all closed. However, they did find a German grocery store in the middle of town. They went in and purchased some local beef and German beer. The town was another one of those towns that looked like at one time it was a busy place to live, but not now. It still was an interesting place to visit.

They received a call from Frank Jr. on the way back to the campground. He told them, Doug and I are coming up to visit you guys tomorrow and we want to stay a week. If you don't have any other plans. Aggie told him; even if we did we would cancel them. Frank asked him, what time do you think you'll be here. Frank Jr. told him we should be there by noon. They both said, "Great, we can't wait!" They hung up, Frank told Aggie I guess we better go home and clean the RV and do laundry. Yeah, I'll go do laundry if you want to clean the house, it won't take long to do it, and then you can take your nap. Frank replied, "Sounds like a plan to me!"

Two hours later, Aggie had the laundry done, and Frank had the RV looking great. When Aggie came home from the laundry, Frank was taking a nap, so she took the girls out for a walk. When she got back Frank was up. Aggie suggested that they surprise the guys and get them a cabin, instead of staying with them in the RV. Frank agreed, Yeah there's not a lot of room for four people in here. Aggie called and there was a cabin open right across from where they were parked.

Frank Jr. and Doug showed up right on time, and Doug had a friend with him, his name was Dax. They were so happy to see the guys. Aggie asked Frank Jr., where are Wanda and Daniel? He told her, they went to look at a couple of colleges for Daniel. Wow, Daniel going to college already? Kids grow-up so fast. Aggie told him. After a little bit, Jr. told them, I want to go up and see if I can get a cabin. Frank smiled at Aggie, can I tell him? Sure! Aggie replied. Frank told Jr., come on I want to show you something. Jr. looked a little confused, what's up? They walked over to the cabin, and Frank handed Jr. the keys, this is your cabin for the week. Cool, how much do I own you? Jr. asked. Frank told him nothing, it's great to spend time with you guys. Jr. went and got his car, Aggie told them, we have everything for dinner. We'll let you guys get settled, come on over when you done.

After about thirty minutes they came back over to the RV. Frank had put out lawn chairs, so they could sit outside and enjoy the cool weather. After a little while, Doug wanted a fire, so they went down and purchased some firewood. It didn't take long to have a blazing fire, and Aggie added some magic coloring crystals to it. It turned the fire into bright blues, purple, dark yellow and deep red. Before you knew it there were kids from the area checking it out. That's all it took for the rest of the week, Doug and Dax had friends to hang out with while they were there.

Aggie found a couple of museums in Sherman, she told the guys about them and they were up to going and checking them out. They picked the Harber Wildlife Museum, to go to first. It was suppose to have about 400-450 animals from all around the world. According to their website, it was opened in 2011, and the owner's were the former American Bank of Texas owner Lacy Harber and his wife Dorothy.

"Dorothy and Lacy have been big game hunters for many, many years — about 30-35 years," museum education director Keith McBrayer said. "Dorothy always hated that she would go to these places and sees all of these animals, but when she returned, there was no way for people to see them here. Most of the kids in this area never get a chance to see these things. They could go to a zoo, but the animals are behind bars. They are off in the distance. You cannot get close to them at all. She always wanted to have a museum so that people could see what they looked like in their natural settings. Of the animals at the museum, McBrayer said the Harbers shot many of them. Dorothy Harber is a dead shot with a bow and arrow."

"Most people think the Harbers brought the animals here," McBrayer said. "But a lot of them they have hunted over the years. Some of these animals used to be in the American Banks. When they moved the animals from the banks, they came here. The polar bear was in the main branch of the bank. Several were at their house. Several were in storage."

"Two of the animals in the museum were not hunted. The Siberian tiger and the white lion were donated to the museum. The Siberian tiger is an endangered species," McBrayer said. "It was in a zoo. It got a kidney infection. They did everything they could, but he got worse. When it seemed like he was getting close to the end someone that knew the Harbers advocated for them to get him after he died. The museum lawyer had to do stacks and stacks of paperwork on him just because he is endangered." Aggie was glad they haven't shot the tiger or lion; it would be terrible to kill them.

They arrived at the museum and the gentleman at the desk explained there are ten sections: "Africa; the wetland; the aquatic area; resources; artifacts; the Asia, Russia, and Australia section; Sundowner room; the desert; the theater; and North America." He gave them a scavenger hunt sheet. Doug and Dax took on the challenge. It was a good way for them to learn about the animals and plants. Of course, everyone got involved in the search. It was fun, things that they normally wouldn't have spotted otherwise. It even had insects and snakes there.

As they were finishing up the tour, the gentlemen they had met earlier started talking to them and told them the nice thing about the museum is, "You can get close to a lion, tiger, and bear. People always ask if the animals are real. We say that they used to be real. They are real friendly. If they were real they would be chasing us around." McBrayer has been with the museum since it opened. As the education director, he said that he enjoys learning about the animals.

It took a little longer then they thought it would take, so they didn't go to the second museum, maybe next time. On the way home they stopped and picked up some chicken at the Golden Chicken. The best chicken around as far as Aggie and Frank were concern. After eating the guys all had to agree with them.

Doug and Dax's friends came over and asked if they wanted to go to the pool, they looked at Frank Jr. and he said sure. We'll all go; he turned and looked at his parent. Aggie said, sure why not, and Frank just smiled and said I guess we're going swimming.

Aggie told the boys that they would meet them over at the swimming pool, after they took the dogs for a walk and put their swimming suits on. Okay, Jr. said, see you there, as they walked over to their cabin.

When Frank and Aggie showed up at the pool the guys were having a great time. There was a bunch of kids and they were playing Marco Polo and diving for objects. There was too many kids to do any swimming so Aggie and Frank got in and got wet and then got back out and watched the kids. It was a beautiful sunny day, not too hot and not too cold.

After about an hour Aggie told the guys they were going to go for a walk. Frank needed to get more walking in, he's been slacking off the last two days. He had good reason, but still he needed to walk.

Aggie had pulled some steaks out for dinner and was marinating them. The cabin had a bigger barbecue so they would have dinner over at the cabin. Aggie and Frank rounded up all the things they needed for dinner and headed over to the camp ground at 5:30 PM. The guys were in the backyard playing Red light, Green light, while they had a fishing pole in the pond. Of course, all the neighborhood kids were there too.

After sending the kids home, Frank Jr. got the BBQ ready. Aggie fixed the baked potatoes and corn on the cob. Frank told Jr., this is the most we have eaten for dinner in quite a while. Normally, we eat a large lunch and then at dinner time something lite.

While they were eating, Aggie told the guys about a Diamond field they could go to tomorrow in Arkansas. According to the website whatever you find you get to keep. There was just a small fee to go in. She pulled out a flier, and started to read: "It is finder keepers at the Crater of Diamonds State Park in Murfreesboro, Arkansas. The only public diamond mine in the world, Crater of Diamonds offers you a one-of-a-kind adventure - the opportunity to hunt for real diamonds and to keep any mineral you find. You'll search over a 37-acre plowed field - the eroded surface of an ancient, diamond-bearing volcanic pipe. Begin your diamond hunting adventure at the visitor center featuring geological exhibits and an audio/visual program that offers a bit of education and explains the area's geology and offers tips on recognizing diamonds in the rough."

She told them, it's about 160 miles away. Are you guys up for a long ride? They all agreed that they were. Aggie said we'll need to leave by 9 o'clock so we have plenty of time there. Jr. said, "We'll be there with bells on."

After visiting a little while and watching a movie it was time to head home. As they were walking back to the RV, Frank told Aggie it's a little weird not having Wanda and Daniel here, Aggie had to agree. But it is nice getting to know Jr. and Doug a little better. Dax was a great kid, he followed Doug around. He was younger then Doug, but he acted a lot older then what he was.

The next morning, the guys were there at 9 a.m., ready to go. It took a little over three hours to get to the Crater of Diamonds State Park. They went through Paris, TX and took back roads to cut off some miles. The place was packed; there were people with pull wagons, filled with buckets, tools and even covers. The place was pretty big; it even had a water park. They rented the tools they needed and headed down to the field. It was plowed into rows, so people could dig easier.

They found a place to start digging. It was getting pretty hot, after a couple hours, Frank went back to the car. About an hour later Aggie gave up and went into the visitor center. While in the visitor center, Aggie read about the place.

The Legend of "Diamond John" - Howard Millar, a former operator of a tourist operation at the Crater of Diamonds and an expert on the crater's history, wrote in his book, "It Was Finders-Keepers at America's Only Diamond Mine," that two geologists had studied the crater site for several years before Huddleston found diamonds here. In 1906, Huddleston bought a farm on the site that the geologists had studied and in August of that year, he found two diamonds.

According to Millar, Huddleston "discovered the first diamonds in Arkansas while he was spreading rock salt on his hog farm. He saw some shiny specks in the dirt that he thought might be gold. But instead of gold, he found two stones."

"Huddleston declined an offer from a local bank cashier, who said he would pay Huddleston 50 cents for the stones. Eventually, the stones were sent to a gem expert in New York City and it was determined that they were indeed genuine diamonds."

"Word soon got out about the diamonds and "Diamond John" Huddleston became famous and put Murfreesboro on the map. Thousands of people flocked to the little town, sparking a boomtown atmosphere. In one year, over 10,000 people were turned away from the Conway Hotel in Murfreesboro. Soon after his find, Huddleston sold his farm for $36,000 and this portion of the crater was closed to the public."

The guys had decided to go panning, after a while they gave up and came to the center. No diamonds were found by any of them, but Aggie found some black jasper. Two were dime side; one was as big a fifty cent piece. She sat in the visitor center waiting for the guys to show up. She was talking to a lady next to her suddenly she started getting woozy. She guessed she didn't look to good either, because the lady asked her "Are you alright?" Aggie replied, I'm a little dizzy, I guess it's from the heat. She offered to get Aggie some water, but Aggie told her she had some, and thanked her. She drank the bottle of water down, and she started to feel better. All she could think of is her fainting and no one would know who she was. She had left her wallet in the car. Frank was in the car, and the guys were still out in the field. She could only imagine being taken off in ambulance, and the guys wouldn't know where she went. Beside's she had the car keys, what a mess that would be. She got up and filled her water bottle and drank that down. About that time Frank came into the center, and the guys came in from the field.

All is well! Aggie asked the guys if they found anything, it was like seeing three little monkeys, see no evil, speak no evil, and hear no evil. Then Doug looked at Dax and said show her! All three had a big smile on their faces, when Dax held up a diamond, it was big but it wasn't a diamond, then he turned to Doug next. Then Doug produced an even bigger diamond. Frank and Aggie turned to Jr. and he produced a little rock that was jasper, this is all I got! He told them. They all started laughing and headed out the door. Jr. told his Mom, this was great fun, too bad it so far away from us. It was getting late so it was time to go. Aggie asked the boys while they were walking back to the car, what are you boys going to do with your diamonds? Both replied, give them to our Moms. Jr. handed Aggie his rock and told her "Mom you can have mine", with a big smile on his face. Oh thank-you sweetheart, I'll keep it forever.

Now for the long drive back, everyone was tired; of course Aggie was pushing the water. She didn't tell the guys about her getting dehydrated, and getting dizzy. After all she was the one always telling people to drink lots of water.

As always the drive back was faster, isn't that the way it is? You go somewhere and it takes forever, and when you go back it seems so much faster. In their case it was, because they got a little lost on the way there. They ended up going though the center of Paris, talk about getting lost. It was Paris, TX! On the way back they stayed on the main road. Paris looked like an interesting town, Aggie wanted to stop and check it out, but the guys all voted her down. Everyone was too tired to cook so they stopped and picked up some chicken, of course from Golden chicken. This time they decided to use the drive thru. Big mistake, when they got home, they found that the order was all mixed up. Fried Okra instead of green beans, corn on the cob missing, and a gallon jug of regular tea, instead of sweet. Lesson learned; always go in to the place to order your order food.

The rest of the week, they just hung around the park and went for a couple of short rides. Jr. and the boys just enjoyed doing nothing, hanging out at the pool and going fishing. It was good to see Jr. enjoying himself; it looked like the boys were having a great time too.

It was hard to see them go, but they were moving tomorrow and heading to Tennessee. They packed up the outside things the day before. They now had four cacti and two flower pots of mums. They have been with them the whole time. It just felt more like home with plants around.

They headed out around 10 a.m., and headed east into Arkansas. Their plan was following the 2x2x2 plan. There was a Thousand Trails in the west end of Tennessee and one in the middle about 80 miles south of Nashville. They were only going to stay two weeks in each place, neither one of them have ever been to Tennessee before.

They stopped twice in Arkansas; one was at a Fair Park RV campground in Hope, AR. There was a horse show going on, which had some nice looking horses. The next morning they headed down the road and got as far as Delta Ridge RV, Forrest City, AR. It was right off the highway. It was a little hard to find the entrance, there was construction going on in the area. But once they found it, it was a really nice place. It was self serve, and reasonably price. The owner did stop by and asked them how everything was going. They stayed two nights, so Frank could rest up.

Next stop Tennessee, good thing to, Frank was getting pretty worn out. He did just have heart surgery, after all. What a man, he could have just stayed put, but he pushed forward. The GPS ended up taking them to Memphis and straight down into Mississippi. They ended up going down every back roads in North Mississippi, it seemed. The roads got smaller and smaller, but Frank just kept going forward. Then all of a sudden out of the blue there was the highway. Ten miles more and they were in Tennessee, they continued toward Cherokee Landing. Aggie radioed Frank to turn, but he kept going. Aggie radioed to him, where are you going? By then he had stopped the RV, and replied back it didn't look like the right road. I'll be right there. In his defense it really didn't look like the right turn. If you're coming from the west, it looks like it's someone's driveway, and there are no Thousand Trails signs, just a little blue sign that says, "Cherokee Landing." From there the campground is still a mile and a half on down the road.

CHAPTER 13

Exploring Tennessee

First stop was Cherokee Landing in the heart of Hardeman Country. According to the book, it is a 250-acre campground nestled in the woods. Aggie took the lead going up the road, they were getting use to TTN always had long roads to get into their sites. The GPS told Aggie they had arrived at their destination, but when she looked around, all that was there was an old building. She wasn't too sure now about this road. There was no place for Frank to turn the RV around either. If she was wrong about it being the road they were supposed to be on. But she just kept driving as she came around the corner there it was, the entrance way to the campground. She really didn't what to hear it from Frank.

They called the Ranger on the radio and in no time at all they were there. The Ranger told them that a nice site with full hook up, it had just opened up that morning; she told them how to get there. Within thirty minutes, they were all settled in, and had dinner. After dinner they took the girls for a long walk, and explored part of the campground. There were two large lodges and a nice size swimming pool. There was also lots of room to go on walks. There were two nice ponds that you could walk around and a long bridge to walk across. After getting back to their site, they were ready to crawl in to bed and watch TV. The girls had no problem with that, they even beat they into bed.

The next day they hung around the campground and Frank got to take a nap, of course the girls had to take one with him. Aggie watched a little TV and wrote in her journal. She wondered if some day someone would read her story about their travels. If nothing else when they couldn't travel anymore, she can read them. She went on line to see what they could go check out tomorrow. She found a few places to go the National Bird Dog Museum, and Ames Plantation to start off with. She told Frank about them and he agreed to go check them out tomorrow.

As they were walking the dogs that morning, they ran into one of the Rangers. Aggie asked her about the Ames Plantation and the Dog Museum. She told them that both were interesting. "In October they have a Fall Heritage Festival, at the Plantation. They show the way things were done back in the old days. Such forgotten skills as farming, knitting, quilting, cooking, goat milking, picking cotton, soap making, tobacco making, etc., it is really something to see."

"They also have a one room schoolhouse, where senior citizens tell old stories for the young ones. The Amish come to make clothing and musical instruments. There is an old chuck wagon that actually has a big pot full of beans and ham, corn fritters, and kettle corn. There's handmade jewelry, antebellum dresses, bluegrass music, and horseshoeing." The rest of the year they have different activities. They also work with Dog Museum and have a hunt every year.

Aggie found this online; "Ames Plantation, home of the National Field Trial Championship for All-Age Bird Dogs, is privately owned and operated by the Trustees of the Hobart Ames Foundation as Successor Trustees under the Will of the late Julia C. Ames. Ames Plantation also functions as one of the University of Tennessee's Ag Research and Education Centers."

"Ames Plantation encompasses 18,400 acres of land in Fayette and Hardeman counties in West Tennessee and is located approximately 60 miles east of Memphis and 10 miles north of the Tennessee-Mississippi line near Grand Junction, Tennessee. The Plantation has approximately 12,000 acres of forest, 2,000 acres of commodity row-crops, and maintains about 300 head of Angus beef cattle and 40 head of horses."

Frank told Aggie lets go check it out, she agreed. We'll see you at the pot luck on Friday, Aggie told the Ranger. They toke the girls back to the RV and headed to the Plantation. As they passed the Dog Museum, Aggie suggested to Frank, let's stop on the way back. He smiled and said sounds good to me, since you already have passed it.

It didn't take long to reach the plantation; it was only about 20 miles from camp. There were field of crops on both sides of the road. They figured it must be cotton. As they came around the corner they saw the old Plantation house, it was huge, and beautiful. There were large Oak trees around it and other out buildings, to the right of it. They saw signs for the office, and followed them. On the right there were old wooden building and a pond. They turned to the left toward the office, and there was another huge pond off to the right and a large barn.

They went into the office and there was a lady at the desk. She welcomed them, and explained they could walk around the grounds, but the Plantation house is only open on the third Thursday of each month. She told them it is still a working plantation, and the house gets used during the National Field Trial Championship for Dogs. They thanked her and went out to walk the grounds. Aggie asked her what are all the crops in the fields are. She told her soybeans, they used to be cotton, but there is more money in soybeans.

There was a small family cemetery just behind the office building; they walked over to check it out. Aggie told Frank; according to their web site they have "Found numerous cemeteries for many of the area's 19th century residents. Of all the historic sites found on the Ames property the cemeteries hold a position of special importance, especially to those who are descended from these earlier occupants." The cemetery they were standing in was the John W. Jones Family Cemetery. The historical marker read: "Established in 1827, this cemetery served as the family buried plot of the Jones family. Twenty-one gravestones mark the burial site of 26 individuals who were a part of the extended Jones family. Investigation of the site has revealed the presence of as many as six unmarked graves. One of the gravestones is Collattinus Jones, located in the cemetery that was burial on January 7, 1827 represents the earliest documented burial in Fayette County."

There were some beautiful head stones; John had the biggest one, and then his wife had the next largest one. There were six children buried here too, all under the age of two. Some of the graves had these oval cement things on top of their graves. They were about 6 inches high; they figured it may have been to mark the graves. They have seen graves with slabs on them before, but nothing like this. One thing about going to old grave yards, you never know what you're going to see.

They went over to where the log cabins were they figured it must be where they have their October event. Talks about how well built the buildings were. They looked like the cabins you see that hillbillies lived in, from the movies. They even had one building with a cabin on each end of the building and a porch in the middle. The cabins it turned out were once used to quarter the slaves before the civil war, and then used after the war by share croppers. They couldn't look inside, but it still was interesting. They wandered around for a little while, and decided to go check out the dog museum on their way home.

When they arrived at the National Bird Dog Museum, and the Field Trial Hall of Fame, workman was pouring cement at the front door. A lady came over to them, and Aggie asked if they were closed. She told them no, just go in over there, she pointed at the side door. There will be a lady to meet you, to show you around.

As they walked into the building, the lady greeted them. She suggested that they go up front and she'll walk them though the museum and explained the different sections. As they were walking along, the lady told them that, "West Tennessee has a rich sporting dog heritage. Geographically, the area is recognized as the birthplace of America's pointing dog field trials, and as the home of the century-old National Field Trial Championship. It is an important hub for bird dog enthusiasts the world over. Its proximity to the Mississippi flyway attracts many waterfowl hunters and others with retriever breed interests."

It was an amazing place, it was much larger than it looked like from outside. They continued to walk, and she pointed out the different breeds, and the awards on display. After they walked though it, the lady told them to go ahead and check it out. If they had any questions just let her know she'll be up front. She also asked them to tell her when they were going to leave. As they wandered around they were both amazed by all the different breeds and awards. They even had a wild life room, which had stuffed small animals. There were more than pictures and painting of forty breeds of bird dogs on display, including pointing, flushing, and retrieving breeds. The tour guide explained that in the beginning the museum just had pointers. As time has gone on each breed club, donated funds to have a section dedicated to their breed.

When they first passed the museum on their way to the campground, it didn't make since why it would be out in the middle of nowhere. But now it does, because the biggest events happened out at the nearby Ames Plantation which is just down the road from Grand Junction, Tennessee. It is only about fifteen miles from the Plantation.

The next day it was time to do laundry, they had checked around in Middleton and Grand Junction, and neither one of them looked all that great. So Aggie went to the one on the campground. It wasn't all that great either, three washers and three dryers; one of the dryers was broken. The laundry was in a long narrow room, with nothing to do while washing except sit outside, because it was too hot in the room. Aggie ended up taking pictures of the different bugs, and posting them on face book to pass the time.

For the next couple of days they went for drives, they found a town called Moscow, TN. "It was the site of a skirmish during the Civil War on December 4, 1863. Confederate cavalry under the command of Gen. Stephen D. Lee attempted to burn the railroad bridge over the Wolf River, in order to aid Gen. Nathan Bedford Forrest in returning to Tennessee from Mississippi. They were thwarted by African-American Union troops who were stationed nearby. Three thousand Confederate cavalry with artillery, led by Gen. James Chalmers, attacked the Memphis & Charleston Railroad Bridge over Wolf River and ambushed Col. Edward Hatch's brigade of Union cavalry crossing the river on the state line road bridge. Intense fighting ensured and fortified Union artillery bombarded the confederate from the rear. Union losses were 175 men and 100 horses. Near sunset the Confederates withdrew, with a loss of 30 killed and 54 taken prisoner. Later the Yankees burned the town of Moscow, leaving only two residences. "

Union Gen. Stephen A. Hurlbut wrote of these troops in a dispatch dated December 17, 1863: "The recent affair at Moscow, Tennessee, has demonstrated the fact that colored troops, properly trained and disciplined, can and will fight well."

Not far down the road was La Grange, where there was more history, and a ceremony, that was turned into an Arboretum. As they walked around they found all kinds of different head stones, some were so old they couldn't read the names or dates on them. Others were large, at least eight foot high. Many were from the Civil War, and others were family plots. Aggie pointed out to Frank the large sea shell on some of the graves, it didn't make sense. Other family plots had iron fencing around them, others iron fencing had nothing inside. They guessed that the people buried there, a long time ago, long enough for their head stones to disappear. It was always interesting to see the history of cemeteries. They had a flier of the Arboretum with a list of all the 65 trees that are planted in the cemetery. There was no printed history of the cemetery on the flier that Aggie found at the cemetery.

They had been at this campground for two weeks, and were running out of things to check out. Aggie was planning the trip to the next site, and suggested to Frank they should go check out the direction the Goggle map suggested. It showed three different ways. Frank agreed with her, they are all about the same distance, it came down to which road looked like the easiest route.

The next morning they headed down the road to check out the different roads. The first one was highway 57, as they were driving along Frank spotted a sign that said, "Shiloh Battlefield." Frank was surprised he didn't know that battle was in Tennessee. Aggie said, well let's go check it out, so she turned and off they went to Shiloh. There was a Civil War store/museum, on the right that they stopped at. It had all kinds of items from the battlefield. Frank had always been interested in the Civil war. His great grandpa was shot in the Pea Ridge battle in Arkansas.

After the museum they followed the signs to the Shiloh Battlefield National Monument. They went into the Battlefield museum where a Ranger greeted them. He told them they were going to show a movie about the battle in 15 minutes. It is a reenactment of the Shiloh battles. It sounds interesting so they decided to go and watch it. It was only going to take about 30 minutes.

The movie was out of the ordinary, and extremely well done. It made you feel like you were there; it was hard to believe how much hardship the soldiers all had to go through. It didn't matter which side you were on, the museum and the reenactment played both sides equally. It showed both points of view, there were no political viewpoints.

As they walked out of the theater, Aggie told Frank I'll never look at the forest the same again. Can you imagine running though the forest in the dark trying to shoot at somebody or being shot at. Not knowing where you're going or what to do. Frank agreed it had to be a nightmare for all of them.

The brochure that they got at the museum explains a small part of what happen there:

"The Battle of Shiloh was the bloodiest battle in American history up to that time. It was eventually superseded that coming September by the Battle of Antietam (an overall bloodier battle, and still the bloodiest single-day in American military history), then the next year by the Battle of Chancellorsville, and, soon after, the three-day Battle of Gettysburg, which would prove to be the bloodiest overall battle of the war."

"Battle of Shiloh was the most epic struggle in the Western Theater of the Civil War. Nearly 110,000 American troops clashed in a bloody contest that resulted in 23,746 casualties; more casualties than in all of America's previous wars combined."

"The Battle of Shiloh, also known as the Battle of Pittsburg Landing. It was fought April 6–7, 1862, in southwestern Tennessee. A Union force known as the Army of the Tennessee, under Major General Grant had moved via the Tennessee River deep into Tennessee and was encamped principally at Pittsburg Landing, TN on the west bank of that river, where the Confederate Army of Mississippi, under General Johnston and second-in-command P.G.T. Beauregard, launched a surprise attack on Grant's army from its base in Corinth, Mississippi."

"Johnston was mortally wounded during the fighting; Beauregard, who thus succeeded to commander of the army, decided against pressing the attack late in the evening. Overnight Grant was reinforced by one of his own divisions stationed further north and was joined by three divisions from another Union army under Maj. Gen. Buell. This allowed them to launch an unexpected counterattack the next morning which completely reversed the Confederate gains of the previous day."

"On April 6, the first day of the battle, the Confederates struck with the intention of driving the Union defenders away from the river and into the swamps of Owl Creek to the west. Johnston hoped to defeat Grant's army before the anticipated arrival of General Buell's Army of the Ohio. The Confederate battle lines became confused during the fierce fighting, and Grant's men instead fell back to the northeast, in the direction of Pittsburg Landing."

"A Union position on a slightly sunken road, nicknamed the "Hornet's Nest," defended by the men of Brig. Gens. Prentiss's and Wallace's divisions provided critical time for the remainder of the Union line to stabilize under the protection of numerous artillery batteries. Wallace was mortally wounded when the position collapsed, while several regiments from the two divisions were eventually surrounded and surrendered. General Johnston was shot in the leg and bled to death while personally leading an attack. Beauregard, his second in command, acknowledged how tired the army was from the day's exertions and decided against assaulting the final Union position that night."

"Tired but unfought and well-organized men from Buell's army and a division of Grant's army arrived in the evening of April 6 and helped turn the tide the next morning. The Union commanders launched a counterattack along the entire line. Confederate forces were forced to retreat from the area, ending their hopes of blocking the Union advance into northern Mississippi."

Aggie and Frank were glad they went and saw the movie. They walked over to the US National Cemetery next. As they walked into the cemetery, they could see there was row after row of head stones. Aggie read the sign at the gate, it explained that after the battle, the Union Army brought all the bodies that they found, and buried both Union and Confederate soldiers. Many head stones didn't have a name on them, but they would at least mark what company they were in, if they knew.

After the Cemetery they went on the driving tour of the battlefields, it was done by using your own car. This means you just drive around and then stop at pull offs on the road. Each had a number which matched the flier they got from the gate. They could read about what happened at that site.

There were many stories to be told of the battle that day. As they stopped at the different sites they could envision what the soldiers were doing. Thanks to the movie it all felt so much more real. They pulled into one site where there were 50 civil war cannons lined up as they were in the battles, which was called Hornets Nests. After watching the movie, Frank and Aggie both imagined what it was like there. The tree line where the Confederates were waiting to attack from wasn't that far from the cannons. Aggie asked Frank, I wonder why they didn't move, when they saw all the cannons being moved in front of them. Frank replied I have no clue why they didn't get out of the way. As they continued around the loop, there were huge statues and monuments throughout the tour. There was one at each battle and they indicated companies that fought there. There also were statues of the Generals and soldiers that were there. Whether you like history or not this is a place to learn and respect our country and the soldiers that were fighting for what they believe.

The central focus during the battle was the Shiloh Log Church, which was used for a hospital on both sides. The Shiloh Log church was built in 1851, it was named after a biblical term for "Place of Peace." The battle was fought over the high ground the church was sitting on. It was a small log cabin, with wooden benches inside. There was another Cemetery across the road from the church. They went over to check it out; there were many head stones from the Civil war. Some had Confederate flags on them. There was so much history in this area. After leaving the battlefield, Aggie saw the sign to Pickwick Dam, she had read a little about it.

"The Pickwick dam is 113 feet high and stretches 7,715 feet across the Tennessee River. During the Great Depression, the towns of Waterloo and Riverton were sacrificed as a result of the construction of the Pickwick Dam. It was more than a loss of property; it was a sacrifice of community for the greater good. This act resulted in a better region allowing for the creation of jobs, economic security, recreational facilities and a better quality of life for the residents of the Tennessee Valley. As in other lost towns throughout the region, these communities and the families that lived in them dedicated their properties, homes and histories to the creation of a vastly improved region and a stronger nation for their children and grandchildren."

They drove over the bridge, and stopped at the state park at the other end of the bridge. In the parking lot there was a huge turbine standing on its end. The kind used in the dam, this was one of the original ones. It stood at least 15 high and the propeller was a good 24 feet diameter.

It was time to head back, Aggie told Frank; it was a good thing that we checked out the route. Frank agreed it's amazing how many road numbers are on these roads, we could have ended up taking the long way to the next site.

On the way back to camp, they heard that a hurricane was headed to the Texas coast. It was named Harvey. Once they got back to camp, they called the kids. They all lived around the Houston area, the girls lived up in the mountain area, but Frank Jr. and their house was close to the bay. Their house was built on stilts; Jr. told them they had boarded the windows up and moved everything into the barn, including their boat. They felt better after talking to Jr., but they kept an eye out on the hurricane. A couple of days later it was time to move to the next site. Jr. told them not to come back toward Texas, just in case the hurricane hit Houston.

They were not going that far, they were going to another Thousand Trails; it was located in central Tennessee. It is called Natchez Trace; it was in the Appalachian Mountains by Lake Hartwell. The drive was nice, they went straight to the site, they were only a half mile away when Aggie drove under a bridge, and she was leading Frank in. She got a call from Frank, he told her, "I can't go under the bridge, it's too low, it's only 11 feet high, and the RV is 12 feet high. She radioed him back; it looks like your clearing it by about a foot. Come on, and I'll keep a watch. As Frank started driving under the bridge, the foot became six inches, just as he got to the second air conditioner, under the bridge, Aggie radioed Frank to stop, but it was too late, he was already under the bridge. There was no light in between the bridge and the RV. Aggie continued to watch, and held her breath. Then there was light again between the bridge and RV. After he was in the open again, Frank radioed Aggie back that was a close one, all I heard hit is the radio antenna.

Something always happens when they travel; this one could have been a big one. It was a good thing Frank watched out for the height of the bridges, as Aggie never did. She was glad that he paid attention to those types of things.

They pulled into the Natchez Trace campground; it had 830-acres in the wilderness just off the Natchez Trace Parkway. They checked in, and found a place in the back part of the grounds. From what they heard on the radio Harvey was headed to the Gulf of Mexico, maybe even hit Houston area. There wasn't much they could do but watch the news. Where they had parked the RV, they couldn't get any cell service, or wifi, if they wanted to call anyone they had to go up to the top of the hill.

The next day they had to go to Nashville; Frank had an appointment at the VA Hospital for his three month check up. It was 80 miles away, and the rain had already arrived from hurricane down in Texas. Everything went well at the doctors; it took a little walking from the parking garage to find out where to go. But the staff was really helpful. It was much shorter walk going back to the car, now that they knew how to go. Soon they were back on the road, but the traffic was getting heavy, because the rain had started Aggie figured.

For the next couple of days the rain was coming down in buckets. According to the news, Texas was getting hit pretty hard by Harvey. She called the kids to find out how things were going. Maria had moved up to some friends of hers, who lived in land. Twilla said it was pretty windy and the rain was coming down pretty hard. But so far they were ok. Jr. said the water is getting pretty close, but so far they are ok too.

Jr. called to give them an update after the storm had passed. Aggie asked if his house was still there. He told her that the water was up to the driveway. They had sandbags everywhere they could think of to stop the water from coming into the house. Frank told Jr. they really needed to get to a safe place until it was all over with. Jr. told them that Wanda and the boys had already left and he was helping some neighbors out before he left. Aggie told him to call them when he gets to wherever he was going.

After a couple days of watching the news about what was going on in Texas. They got another call from Frank Jr. he told them that everyone was fine but Frank and Aggies's house had at least two feet of water around it. It was a good thing that they had their RV; otherwise it would have been washed away. They had opened up the canal and it had flooded the whole area.

Frank thanked him for letting them know about their house, there is not much we can do about it right now. We're just glad everyone is ok, and your house is ok. After they got off the phone, Frank turned to Aggie and said, at least we had put our things in storage, and that Penelope (RV) wasn't parked in the flood zone.

Just before and after Harvey came in they saw RV's with Texas license plates, there were 30 or more in the park for about a week, and then they disappeared. Aggie had talked to a few of them, one had been in a few floods, and wanted to get as far from the flooding as they could. Another of them told Aggie that the hurricane hit their house straight on and there wasn't much left of it. A friend had sent some pictures of their place; the stilts were still there, some piles and the storage room that was made out of cement blocks, where they put all of important things they couldn't get into the trailer.

Sally told her, if you live in that area, you become aware of the most important things in life. Of course your children and pets, but pictures are so important. She told Aggie, they have a water/fire proof chest they always have their pictures in. Everything else is only secondary. Aggie agreed with her, and told her they had a house in Houston too. They had packed everything up before they left and put it in storage on the other side of town. Just in case something like this happens. You never know what kind of weather you'll get in Houston.

Aggie had a brochure about the Natchez Trace Parkway, it looked very interesting. "The Natchez Trace Parkway is 444 miles long. It goes through three states and 10,000 years of history. It's been a National Park since 1938 and the parkway was completed in 2005. It commemorates the most significant highway of the Old Southwest. It roughly follows the "Old Natchez Trace" a historic travel corridor used by American Indians, "Kaintucks," European settlers, slave traders, soldiers, and future presidents."

The brochure had the full length map of the parkway, all 444 miles of it, and the different point of history on the trail. There is 110 miles in Tennessee. Aggie wanted to at least travel the TN section, Frank agreed it would be interesting according to the brochure. The next couple of weeks they explored the different sites. There were many hiking trails, and lots of people riding their bikes. The road was a two lane, and in great shape.

Frank and Aggie decided to go south first and cross into Mississippi. The first stop going south was Collinwood, TN. It had a visitor center there, which was being run by senior citizen volunteers, and all were very friendly. There was a small museum in the center; it showed the history of the town.

According to the information from the museum, "Collinwood was established in 1913 as a stop on the Tennessee Western Railroad, a rail line constructed to serve the area iron industry. The Collinwood Land

Company advertised lots for the new city in June 1913, and by the following year, about 300 people were living in the town. Most of the residents worked for the railroad or in the local lumber industry. During World War I, Collinwood's economy boomed, and its population swelled to over 2,000. A wood alcohol (methanol) distillation plant and blast furnace were constructed in the years following the war, but as demand for these products fell, the economy collapsed and the city began to decline. The tracks connecting Collinwood with the L&N system were abandoned in the late 1930s."

On the way down to Mississippi there were a few more pull offs: McGlamery Stand, Sunken Trace, and Holly were picnic area, there was information panels at these sites, but not much else. They stopped at the State line where they took a couple of pictures, next to the sign. It was a sign to mark the state line. On the sign it showed the state seals of both states and a short history of how the states were separated.

The next stop Mississippi; they crossed over Tennessee River where there was a state park on the other side of the bridge, on the river, and another history lesson.

They found a park by the river with picnic tables and an area to walk the dogs and have lunch. There weren't very many people around, just a mother with her toddler daughter, and a guy with his German Sheppard, which wasn't on a lease. The owner of the Sheppard really wasn't paying attention to his dog; he was on the phone talking. The mother and the little girl were coming down the path out of the woods, when the Sheppard ran over to them. The mother put the little girl behind her, and yelled at the dog to go away. The little girl was still hiding behind her mother when she finally got the dog to go away. Frank and Aggie looked over at the owner and he was clueless. She took the little girl hand, and walked as fast as she could to get away from the dog.

After a little bit the Sheppard started getting closer to Frank and Aggie, and still not on a lease. The owner still was clueless. As the dog started to get closer to them, Aggie started yelling at the owner, "Hey, Hey can you call your dog;" he looked at her like she was crazy. She yelled at him again, you do know your suppose to have the dog on a lease? That must have gotten his attention. He called his dog, and a few minutes later they were gone.

After being attacked by "Nice dogs" three times, Aggie wasn't going to take anymore changes. They sat and watched the ships and barges go by for awhile, when the mother and daughter stopped by, and petted their little dogs and then left.

Well it was time to move on, as they were leaving the park, Aggie saw a historical sign, pointing down the road, she turned the car toward it. The first sign was about "George Colbert who was a Chickasaw Chief. He operated a ferry across the Tennessee River from 1800 to 1819. His stand or Inn offer travelers a warm meal and shelter during their journey on the

Old Trace road. Colbert looked after his own well-being and once charged Andrew Jackson 75,000 dollars to ferry his Tennessee Army across the river." They walked up the path to see where the Inn used to be. There they found another information panel that was about Colbert.

"During the early 1800s, George Colbert's family, emerged among the Chickasaw, he was a slave owner in the planter class (plain folks). George's success stemmed from a variety of endeavors. He fought with the Americans against the Shawnee and Creeks. He established the Colbert's ferry near Cherokee, Alabama. Colbert accumulated land and became a powerful planter. He owned est. 150 slaves. His economic and political power enabled him and his brothers to be among the primary negotiators of treaties between the Chickasaw people and the United States government."

"In the late 1830s, Colbert and many of his fellow Chickasaw were moved to Oklahoma under the Indian Removal Act. He married three times, and fathered six sons and two daughters."

Aggie told Frank, Old George was something else, charging $75,000 to use his ferry, that's a lot of money at the time. The fact that he was a slave owner is pretty wild. I never thought about Indians having slaves. Frank agreed, as they walked back to their car, Frank said, can you imagine all of the soldiers, horses and wagons waiting in line to get on the ferry. It would have been crazy.

Aggie had to agree with him as they got in the car. The girls settled down in their beds, and before too long they were sleeping. Today the campground was changing the gate code. They figured they would get it when they came back. As it turned out there was no one in the Ranger station, which was no big deal, Aggie called them on the radio, but there was no answer, she waited a couple of minutes and tried again still no response. She decided to go to the campground store and see if they could help them. But they couldn't give out the pass code. They tried to get the Ranger on the radio, but they had no luck either, so the store clerk called the main office. She got an answer, she told them about no one at the Ranger station. They said they would be right there and asked her to tell Aggie and Frank to meet them there. They went back to the gate and the lady was there. She apologized, and told them she wasn't sure where Susi was. She gave them the new code and Aggie and Frank headed home. By now the girls were awake and ready to go for another walk.

The weather was starting to change; Hurricane Irma was hitting the South Florida. It was strange seeing so many rigs coming from Florida. According to the Ranger, they had 70 reservations coming from Florida, for the next couple of days. Frank was talking to one of the new neighbors and he told Frank, this was the first place that still had openings. If Irma hits like they said, even here their going to feel her. Everyone in the resort where they lived had gone or was leaving. Where he lived he said it was right on the west side of Florida, not far from the ocean. They did have friends that did stay behind, but they were in a cement house not in a trailer. For the next couple of days they saw rigs coming in from Florida, a few were neighbors in Florida, and were traveling together.

Aggie wanted to finish the Natchez Trace Parkway, well the North end anyway. The map showed there was a lot to see, and they were told that there was a really good restaurant at the end of the trail. They had driven by the Meriwether Lewis memorial a couple of times. But this time they were going to stop and check it out.

They left the girls at home this time, it was going to be a warm day, and they didn't what to leave them in the car. It was time to go explore, which is Aggies's favorite thing to do. First stop was Laurel Hill Lake, it was about five miles off the road, but it was worth the drive. It had cabins and a nice fishing area, and they could rent a boat if they wanted. By the looks of it, there were lots of fish, as they sat and looked over the water. They could see fish jumping up out of the water. Everything in the park was closed; it was only open on the weekend during the winter.

Time to head up the road; they stopped at a rest area, which had a picnic area down in the ravine but it was what they spotted across the ravine that got their attention. It was a cemetery; there was nothing about it on the map and no signs either. We should go check it out Aggie suggested to Frank; he agreed but suggested to stop on the way back. She agreed and marked it on the map so they didn't miss it on the way back.

They reached Meriwether Lewis Monument, there was a cabin there called the Old Grinder House, it is where Meriwether Lewis took his own life on the night of Oct 11, 1809. Aggie was surprised to hear he had killed himself, not only that but he had tried a few times before. Near the cabin they had a head stone but they were not sure whether he was buried there.

They stopped at a few more areas on their way up the Trace, one was an Old Tobacco Farm, the information sign said: It was a typical early 1900's tobacco farm. There were tobacco plants growing to the left and an old barn to the right. Neither one of them had ever seen a live tobacco plant. They were huge broad leaves plants, about four feet high. Then they walked over to the barn, where they used to dry the leaves. There were signs explaining the process. They used the stalks of the plant to hang it upside down, and then strip the leaf off of the stalks, after they were dried out. It was interesting; the tobacco plant is called "Burley". Learn something new every day, Aggie told Frank.

Back on the road it wasn't far before they pulled off again at the next stop, which was a rest area too. It was the Gordon House; you could see it from the parking lot. It was just a short walk to check it out. "The house was a trading post and ferry stop in the 1800's. It's one of the few remaining buildings associated with the Old Natchez Trace. It was the house of ferry operator John Gordon." In the early 1800's Gordon made an agreement with the Chickasaw Chief George Colbert to operate a trading post and ferry on the Duck River.

"Military expeditions with General Jackson kept him away from home much of the time. His wife Dorathea supervised the construction of the present house in 1817-18. John Gordon died shortly after it was completed, but Mrs. Gordon lived in the house until her death in 1859."

Aggie laughed as she was reading it, good old George had his hands in everything around here. It's kind of weird he had so much power, but yet they made him move to Oklahoma Indian territory. The old house was a two story brick building, with two doors on the front side and one on the back side. There are eight windows on the top floor. It was a pretty nice house for being out in the middle of nowhere. Aggie could only imagine what it was like being out there keeping the business going while her husband was out fighting in the war.

They headed on down the road; many of the pull off areas were information panels, and had couple of rest areas. There were a lot of bikes out today. Aggie guess being a Saturday had something to do with it. They finally arrived at the end of the Trace, and found the restaurant that they were told about. It was packed, but they figured they are there so they should try it. Aggie asked, how long is the wait? The hostess told her an hour and 45 minutes. Aggie told her no thanks, we'll go somewhere else. Thanks anyway. The hostess didn't act to surprised. They found another place to eat, and then headed back south on the Trace Parkway. Most of the bikes were gone, after about 25 miles, and the Parkway was pretty much theirs.

They planned on stopping at the cemetery they spotted earlier. They almost missed the turn; it was just a little dirt road. There was no sign on the road pointing toward the cemetery, and as they drove up to it, there was no sign with the name of the cemetery. They got out of the car, and walked over to it, almost all of the graves had fresh piles of dirt on top of them. Just like when someone first got buried. There were flowers on almost all of the graves. Some were buried in the early 1900's and others were buried in 2014. Frank suggested, it must be a family cemetery, but there were so many different names. It was a really unusual place, but someone is keeping good care of it. Oh Well, I guess it's another mystery for us, Aggie said to Frank.

The next few days' the weather left over from Hurricane Irma arrived. Irma had moved toward South Carolina, and that was where they were planning on going to next. After watching the weather and hearing that there were three more hurricanes coming in, they figured it would be better to go North instead of East. Frank told Aggie, well we gave it a shot; we'll have to try again next year. Because of Frank's heart surgery it put them behind a month in their travels. Aggie was just happy his heart issue was discovered before he had a heart attack. If he would have had a heart attack on one of their walks, everything could have been must worse. But everything is good now; they will be back next year to see the East Coast.

Look out Kentucky here they come. They will be doing road trips, which mean they will travel for a half a day, or two hundred miles. Normally, they would just travel to the next Thousand Trails (TTN) and stay for three weeks, then goes to the next one. But there isn't any TTN in the central states. With it costing a $100 a day for gas, and $30 plus a night for a site, it can get a little spend. They also packed things differently when they did road trips. Usually, they would put the storage buckets and plants in the Jeep, but when they do the road trips, they tied down the storage buckets on top of the tool box, which was on the tail of Penelope. Because if they wanted to take the girls with them on a day trip, normally there wouldn't be room in the back for them, this way there was.

CHAPTER 14

Heading back to Texas

T hey plan on traveling through Kentucky, the corner of Illinois, Missouri, Arkansas and Oklahoma. It should take a couple of weeks to get back to Texas. With all of the storms coming in, and their house being flooded, there was no reason to go back to Houston with the RV. Lake Texoma was the closest TTN to them. About a thousand miles away, beside they get to add more States to their map on the side of their RV.

They did a recon the day before, the map showed there was construction on the road they plan on taking, if it looked like a nightmare they would just go the longer way around. The good news it was all done, it looked like an easy drive. Aggie had found a campground in the Passport book just inside of

Kentucky, called Pirates Cove Resort. It was about 7 miles away from the highway, outside a town called Hardin, Kentucky.

As they turned in at the Pirates Cove sign, the road suddenly was getting smaller; Frank hoped no one came down the road. Thank goodness, no one did. Aggie was in the lead, and radioed Frank that it was all clear, and they were in the right place. One thing for sure, those little walkie talkie they purchased five years ago, was one of the best investments they made for traveling.

Frank pulled in next to Aggie, she went to the office where there was a note saying it was only open on the weekend, and today was Thursday. She radioed Frank and told him, he replied back is there a number we can call? I don't see one; let me look around, that was when a man in a pickup truck pulled up to her. He told her he could help her out, he ran the place. He said just follow me and off he went. Aggie watched where he took off to, and radio Frank, "Follow that truck!" so he did and Aggie followed Frank. She was glad the owner showed up, he had explained that he saw them on the camera. JR was his name; he gave Aggie his phone number and said someone will be by later to take the payment.

The campground was right on the lake, it wasn't anything fantastic, but it was quiet, and a great view. Aggie teased Frank, JR gave me his phone number, I guess I might have a date tonight, as she smiled at him. He just laughed and said, "Yea right!" They did a light set up, which is just connecting to the power and water. There was no septic hook up at the site, but there is a dump site on the way out. Aggie had seen on the paper map, there was a place called "Land between the Lakes," she wasn't sure what it meant. Of course, she had to find out why.

It is a "170,000 acre playground in Western Kentucky and Tennessee; it has 300 miles of undeveloped shoreline." The reason why it is called this is: "Land Between the Lakes is an inland peninsula formed when the Cumberland and Tennessee Rivers were impounded, dedicated Kentucky Lake and Lake Barkley. One of the world's largest man-made bodies of water was made. In 1963, President John F. Kennedy created Land between the Lakes National Recreation Area." By the sound of the brochure it is a huge outdoor park, fun for everyone.

There are a few things they wanted to go check out; The Elk & Bison Prairie reserve was one of them the other is the 1850s museum. They just hung around Penelope for the rest of the evening, traveling takes a lot out of Frank, which Aggie understood. Even before the heart surgery, it could be a challenge to drive her (Penelope), with the fools on the road, the wind, and some of the roads that Aggie would get him on. Every time a large truck would go by, Aggie would hold her breath. Some of the states have 70 mph speed limits on the back roads, two lanes, it was crazy sometimes.

The next morning after breakfast they headed toward the Land between the lakes, it was only eight miles away. First stop the Golden Pond Visitor Center; it had the history of the area, and a Planetarium. They didn't go to the Planetarium because there were two school buses full of kids going into the Planetarium. Neither one of them wanted to deal with a bunch of teenagers. After the museum they went over to the Elk and Bison Prairie, it was 700 acres of prairie and a 3.5 mile paved loop. They were hoping to see Bison or Elk. There were pull outs that had information boards with a little bit of history or tell you what to look for. It cost $5 to get into, as they drove the loop, they were watching both sides of the road, hoping to see something. The brochure suggested going early morning or late afternoon. They were there in late afternoon. They drove the loop and didn't see anything, not even a bird; they decided to go around again hoping to see something, they did see a truck and car, and there was a large bird flying about three miles away.

They had to wonder how so many animals can disappear. There was a truck pulled off to the side, so Aggie stopped the Jeep, and Frank asked the driver if they saw anything. He told him no, Frank said same here; we even went around the loop twice. Aggie drove down the road slowly still hoping to see something, but no luck. Aggie suggested they go down by the lake; there was a nice park area where they went. There was a lodge there but it was closed.

It looks like this area is set up for summer, not too much going during the fall. As they were looking over the bridge, they could see large shells on the bank. Aggie had to have them; they found a place they could walk down to the water's edge. There were two sets of fresh water oyster shells. They looked pretty old, another souvenir for their collection. Their collection of shells and rocks is getting pretty big.

It was time to get home, and get ready for the trip tomorrow; it was going to be a little longer day than before. They needed to do one long day to get to Texoma; Aggie had made reservations for the next week. The site will be in the Ozark Mountain Springs, MO, another state to add to their map. The trip was more highway than back roads this time. There were a lot of truck traffic; it was one of the main highways in MO.

But nothing compared to the next part of their journey. Somehow or another they missed a turn and started going the wrong way. But Aggie caught it in time and found a road to put them back on track. They went from Kentucky, to Illinois to Missouri within thirty minutes. When they started crossing the Mississippi River is when it got scary, as far as Aggie was concerned. The bridge was so narrow, and it didn't look possible for two big rigs to pass each other on it.

They arrived at the campground around two p.m.; it looked to be pretty nice. It was another Passport campground, but when they told the owner, he said they didn't take Passport discounts anymore. But they did give a discount to prior services personnel. The reason they try to use Passport at campgrounds is because they could get 50% off.

They were shown to their site, it wouldn't have been a place they would have picked, and because they could see and hear the highway. The truck traffic was all night, but the weird thing was as Aggie and Frank laid in bed they could feel the ground shake a little each time a truck went by. Aggie suggested to Frank, maybe there is a cavern underneath the highway that they haven't found yet.

It was a rough night last night because the thunderstorm came in, which always scare the dogs. So they spent the night trying to calm them down. Their next stop was a little over 200 miles away where they wanted to camp by the Pea Ridge Battleground in Arkansas. Frank wanted to see where his great-grandfather had been wounded. They stopped a few times to take a break to have lunch and let the dogs go for a walk. It was a nice change staying on the highway instead of taking back roads. It was usually shorter to take the back roads than to stay on the freeways. Most of the back roads were two lanes and pretty nice, some of them were a little iffy at times. But Frank could always get through them, while Aggie held her breath.

Then Aggie saw a road sign that had Little Rock, AR 150 miles, this wasn't the way they wanted to go. The GPS had picked the wrong way; there was three ways to get to Lake Texoma. They wanted to go though Missouri and Illinois, so they could add them to their map on the RV. Aggie radioed Frank and told him to pull over, their going the wrong direction. They pulled off to the side of the road, and then Aggie asked for directions to Pea Ridge instead of Lake Texoma on her phone. After a little bit she radioed Frank, and told him to turn right at the next road. They were not too far off, but they were going to have to take back roads again.

After a while they were back on track, and were taking Hwy 57, when they went across the Ohio River, the bridge looked like it had been there awhile. As they were going over the bridge, Aggie noticed that there wasn't too much room between the truck and their RV. As unusual Aggie held her breath until it was over. They drove from AR, KY, and then IL in the last fifteen miles, next they were going over the Mississippi River into Missouri. As Aggie followed Frank over the second bridge, she couldn't believe the bridge was even narrower then the last one and longer. She just hoped no big trucks came over at the same time. Of course, that was not going to happen. The first truck came by, they were so close, and if their mirrors would have been at the same height they would of hit. Frank moved over a little, and his back tire hit the curve. No big deal, Aggie was thinking to herself. Then another even bigger truck was coming, she slowed down the car so she wouldn't be too close to their RV. The trucker was hauling ass, Aggie guessed his done this a few times. As the truck passed Frank there was maybe an inch of light between them.

After they got off the bridge, Aggie made a mental note; they wouldn't come back this way. They would go the long way around. These bridges are crazy! She radioed Frank, how are you doing. He told her fine, but that was one slim bridge, and he was surprised that the truck didn't hit him. She just replied back, there was no room to spare, that's for sure.

They pulled into the campground that Aggie had found in the Passport book. It was an interesting place to say the least. When they pulled up the owner came out and told them that there were no openings, and normally they only did long-term RVer's. They told them that there was a big motorcycle festival going on in that corner of Arkansas. They also told them all of the campgrounds in the area were full because of the festival. They would probably have to go another 100 miles to find a campground that had an opening.

They decided that they were going to go ahead and check out the Pea Ridge Museum and battleground before they headed out again. They could park the RV in the Museum parking lot, and take a little break. Then check out the site.

The problem was that they couldn't leave the dogs in the RV because there was no power for the air-conditioning. So they didn't get a chance to look around the museum. But they did have that drive tour that they went on instead; the dogs just rode with them in the car. There was 11 pull offs, each had their own story to tell. The first one wrote about the "Trail of Tears" where the Chickasaw and other American Indians in the winter of 1838-1839 were forced to leave their homeland.

The information they read about the sign was, "Trail of Tears, in U.S. history, the forced relocation during the 1830s of Eastern Woodlands Indians of the Southeast region of the United States (including Cherokee, Creek, Chickasaw, Choctaw, and Seminole, among other nations) to Indian Territory west of the Mississippi River. Estimates based on tribal and military records suggest that approximately 100,000 indigenous people were forced from their homes during that period, which is sometimes known as the removal era, and that some 15,000 died during the journey west."

"The term Trail of tears invokes the collective suffering those people experienced, although it is most commonly used in reference to the removal experiences of the Southeast Indians generally and the Cherokee nation specifically. The physical trail consisted of several overland routes and one main water route and, by passage of the Omnibus Public Lands Management Act in 2009, stretched some 5,045 miles (about 8,120 km) across portions of nine states (Alabama, Arkansas, Georgia, Illinois,

Kentucky, Missouri, North Carolina, Oklahoma, and Tennessee)."

Frank and Aggie had seen sites in a few of the states, which marked where the Trail of Tears went through. It's a story that Americans try not to remember. They continued on the Pea Ridge Battlefield tour.

The information on one of the sign explained that, "On March 7-8, 1862, 26,000 soldiers fought here to decide the fate of Missouri and the West. The 4,300 acre battlefield honors those who fought for their beliefs. Pea Ridge was one of the most pivotal Civil War battles and is the most intact Civil War battlefield in the United States."

"Pea Ridge was the only major Civil War battle in which Indian troops participated. Two regiments of Cherokees, about 1,000 men, fought for the Confederate Army and routed to companies of Union Calvary. Heavy Union Cannons fire eventually forced them to take cover in the woods. The Cherokee regiments were held in reserves throughout the remainder of the battle."

"They pulled up to where Frank's great-grandfather had been shot, it was called Leetown battlefield. The Confederates attacked through the woods north of the field they were standing in. They failed to defeat the Federals that deployed along the south fence line. Two Confederate generals Ben McCulloch and James McIntosh were killed near the north boundary of the field. There was a small village that stood a short distance southwest of the parking lot."

"During the battle the wounded of both sides were brought here, where buildings and tents served as hospitals. There was nothing left of visible evidence of the village to be seen, there was just an open field there now." Frank's great-grandfather, Andrew Jackson Moulder, could have been in this town too. He was shot in the back, and lived his life with the bullet in his back for the rest of his life. He lived until Nov 28, 1928 and died at the age of 90, (1838-1928).

There was one old building that they stopped at, "it was called Elkhorn Tavern and was described as a place of "abundant good cheer." It served travelers on the telegraph Road before the war came to Arkansas Union. Gen. Curtis used a tavern as part of his supply base until Confederates captured and occupied early in the afternoon on March 7. They turned it into a field hospital occurring for both Union and Confederate wounded. Union troops took the Tavern on March 8 after routing the Confederate forces from the field. The federals used the Tavern as a military telegraph station until the Confederate guerrillas burned it in 1863."

The building was interesting, Aggie could have sworn the building must have been the original but it wasn't, it was a reconstruction of the old one. Inside it had makeshift tables that looked like it had blood stains, and a couple of fire places and ammo boxes.

There was a Ranger there to tell them about the history of the building, and the role that it played in the war.

Frank and Aggie could only imagine how horrible it had to be there for all of the men that were there. One thing about traveling in the south they had seen a lot of different battlefields and the history of the area. They wish they could have stayed longer and visited the Pea Ridge Museum and the other things in the area. But they did need to find a place to stay the night. When they got into the RV it was pretty warm so they opened all the windows before leaving so it would cool off as they drove down the road.

They ended up driving another 80 miles before finding a campground. It was in Alma, AR, the campground was called Fort Smith – Alma RV Park. It was a nice Park, the front part of it was for RVs and the backside was a trailer park. The owners were really friendly and helpful; it was really nice that they were able to stop for the next couple of days.

Alma is the "Spinach Capital of the World." Aggie told Frank I bet you didn't know that. Frank just smiled and said he didn't see any spinach fields but maybe it was too late in the season.

They didn't do much for the next couple of days; they wanted to rest up for the next long-haul. Their plan was to head straight to Lake Texoma, which was 287 miles away.

It was a long drive; they stopped a couple of times on their way. Aggie saw a couple of places she wanted to come back to later. They arrived at Lake Texoma TTN campground. This will be the third time they had stayed here. They found a nice site, it was by the pond, and had a nice size site, a cabin on one site, and a Personnel site on the other. They set up camp and relaxed for the next couple of days. The dogs acted like they remembered the park. Susi even tried to go to the cabin where Jr. and the kids stayed; Aggie guessed she was looking for them.

CHAPTER 15

Checking out Oklahoma

It was going on the third day, and Aggie couldn't stand it any longer, she had been researching what they could do in Oklahoma. The last two times they never really explored the area around them. She planned a day out, starting with Ft. Washita, and then the Chickasaw museums. The Chickasaw nation and their people owned the land in that area.

The Fort sounded like a cool place to check out, and it wasn't too far away. "Fort Washita, OK was built in 1842 and operated through 1865; the fort's purpose was to protect the Chickasaw and Choctaw Tribes from marauding plains tribes. Log structures were built at first, and then permanent native sandstone and refined wooden structures were built."

"Federal forces abandoned the fort at the beginning of the Civil War in 1862. Confederate forces then occupied it and it became a major supply depot for Confederate troops in Indian Territory. In 1962, the fort was acquired by the Oklahoma Historical Society, who restored some of the fort's original structures."

When they arrived at the Fort, there were only a couple of cars there, they went up to the visitor center, and a Chickasaw lady was on the front porch working on something. She had been busy, and she had two large boxes of them. Aggie had to ask her what were they for, she explained that they were called Bogue Gourds. They have short necks, and have a hard shell once you dry them out; they grow on 20' vines and are insect resistant. She was cleaning them out for the annual Chickasaw Nation, "Gathering of the People", event. She was going to teach classes on how to use them. Originally, her people used to use them to store things. But at the gathering, they used them as ornaments. The interesting part was after they were cleaned up they looked a lot like coconuts.

The lady explained that they could walk or drive the tour, she gave them a map. Frank asked if there was a cemetery on the property, she said yes, there is a family owned area, as she pointed in the direction where it was at. Aggie and Frank thanked her, and decided to walk the Fort grounds. It was so quiet there, and an old log cabin stood not far away, so they went over to look at it first, it was well built. On a sign board, there were posters describing the way they punished the soldiers for their different crimes. Aggie read a few of them to Frank.

"Punishments were often creative such as tying two soldiers together for a 24-hour period for the offense of fighting among themselves or saddling a soldier with full saddle and accouterments and marching him around the parade grounds for improper horse care."

"A soldier who reported for roll call improperly dressed might be required to wear a "wooden overcoat" (a barrel without top or bottom) in place of his uniform for a day." They both we're laughing, could you imagine seeing this or even having to do it, Frank asked Aggie. Aggie agreed; listen to this one, "Punishment involved being strung up by one's thumbs, tied spread eagle on a wagon wheel or the ground, marching the punishment line with a knapsack full of rocks, or solitary confinement either in the guardhouse or a hole in the ground. Duration of the punishment was also discretionary for the commanding officer. After serving out his punishment if required the soldier would receive medical treatment, which could be a punishment of its own."

They continued on their walk toward the south barracks. "South Barracks was originally built with wood and bricks, but it was burned to the ground by vandalism in the 1990s, and only walls of the ruins remains." They plan on rebuilding it someday, according to the Ranger.

As they walked up to the Bohanan Cabin, Frank told Aggie there are spirits here. He could feel them, he had the feeling that he should move away from the cabin. Aggie hadn't told Frank about "Aunt Jane" she had read it on line before they came to see the fort.

She told him it must be Aunt Jane. "It is rumored that she haunts here. Aunt Jane was a strong-willed woman who was murdered by thieves sometime before 1861 because she wouldn't disclose the location of her buried money. In a vicious struggle, the thieves beheaded Aunt Jane, and her remains were scattered and buried on Fort Washita. Her money was never found."

"However, her ghost has reportedly been seen floating near the ruins wearing a white gown. Aunt Jane kept a relatively low profile until the late 19th or early 20th century when her spirit allegedly possessed a child named Molly Stalcup who lived near the fort. Aunt Jane threatened to cut off all of the child's hair and only fled after Mrs. Stalcup began praying. That's the last thing that was written about her."

As they walked away the feeling left Frank, they walked around for a little while. Then got in their car and drove to the Confederate Cemetery at the far end of the grounds. The sign at the Cemetery said it had been in use from 1861-1865, 200 unknown soldiers were buried there in a mass grave. There weren't any details in the brochure about this site.

As they were walking around in the cemetery, Frank stopped and saluted the soldiers and their flag. As he was doing that, he could feel their energy come around him. Frank felt very welcome there. One of his ancestries had been on the confederate side during the war; it was seemed like the right thing to do. He told Aggie about the feeling, so Aggie wanted to try something. Their confederate flag was hanging over the mass grave and there was no wind. She asked the soldiers to make their flag fly high. She really didn't think it would happen. Then all of a sudden the flag flew full, and straight as if there was a strong wind, which there wasn't any in the moment before. They both got a cold chill up their spine. As Frank told Aggie, they're here saluting their flag.

As they left the Confederate cemetery, Aggie told the sprits to go toward the light, their families are waiting for them. They got back in the Jeep and wanted to go check out the "Chickasaw White house," the Ranger had told them about earlier. Aggie had asked her about the trees that had the large yellow things; they almost looked like grapefruit with bumps. Aggie and Frank had seen them in a couple different states, but no one they asked knew much about them. The Ranger did know the name of them and that you can't eat the fruit, horses, squirrels and cows love them.

Aggie wrote down the name and she looked it up on line. This is what she found, "The bodark tree (Maclura pomifera) is a common tree in Arkansas.

Funny they were in Oklahoma. They have seen the tree in Tennessee, and Texas also. They have been known to live in at least forty-seven of the state's seventy-five counties. The name "bodark" is a slurring of the French "bois d'arc," meaning "wood of the bow"—a reference to the Osage Indians' practice of making bows from the tree."

"The yellow-green fruit is commonly called "**hedge apples**." They are produced by the Osage-orange (Maclura pomifera). Other common plant names include hedge apple, bodark, bois d'arc, and bowwood. The Osage-orange is a small- to medium-sized tree." Aggie also found out there is a lot of history with this tree. "The earliest account of the tree in the English language was given by William Dunbar, a Scottish explorer, in his narrative of a journey made in 1804 from St. Catherine's Landing on the Mississippi River to the Ouachita River. It was a curiosity when Meriwether Lewis sent some slips and cuttings to President Jefferson in March 1804. According to Lewis's letter, the samples were donated by "Mr. Peter Choteau, who resided the greater portion of his time for many years with the Osage Nation."

"Those cuttings did not survive, but later the thorny Osage orange tree was widely naturalized throughout the United States. In 1810, Bradbury relates that he found two trees growing in the garden of Pierre Chouteau, one of the first settlers of St. Louis, apparently the same person."

"Meriwether Lewis was told that the people of the Osage Nation, "Had so much ... esteem for the wood of this tree for the purpose of making their bows, that they would travel many hundreds of miles in quest of it."

Aggie found much more, she was very surprised how much information there was about the tree. Now if anyone asks her about the fruits lying on the ground she can tell them about the Bodark tree and its history.

The Ranger was a Chickasaw woman, she told them about some other things in the area they should check out. Before they left they wanted to check out the family cemetery at the other end of the Fort. There was only the foundation of the hospital, which was right next to the cemetery. That sure didn't look like a good sign. Aggie pointed at the hospital and then the cemetery. Frank laughed, and said yea, Hey look whose family cemetery this is. Aggie saw that there were Colbert head stones everywhere and told Frank, you got to be kidding. Do you think its George's family? Frank replied, just how many Chickasaw are named Colbert! True, as they walked around they didn't see George's grave, but he did have six sons, so this could be part of his family.

Let's go to the Chickasaw White house, the Ranger was telling us about, Frank said let's go. The information Aggie got from the web site was: "The Chickasaw White House was once considered a mansion on the Oklahoma frontier. The property was the home of Chickasaw Governor Douglas Hancock Johnston and his family from 1898 to 1971. Now under the care of the Chickasaw Nation, the Chickasaw White House has been lovingly restored to its full grandeur, just as it was around 1900. The home contains unusual features for its era including 14-ft ceilings, cherry mahogany fireplace mantels, crystal chandeliers and a dance floor."

They arrived at the White house, about thirty minutes later. A lady came out of the office and asked them if they would like a tour, or just wander around the property. Aggie said they would like the tour. They preferred taking the tour, you can learn more about a place, and the Guides always had extra things to tell you.

The web site was right, it was a beautiful home; much of the furniture was the Governor's furniture. They were a very talented family; their daughter had painted plates, and other things around the house. They also played numerous musical instruments. There was a piano there, but it wasn't the original one, the original one was too big. As they walked around the house, Frank told Aggie there is a strong energy here. Aggie liked having Frank around; he could feel energy/sprits when they were around. Even at old cemeteries, he gets a chill and then he gets goose bumps on his arms. If there are a lot of sprits, he said the energy even feels stronger. She's always asking Frank if he feels anything in an area where someone may have died.

Aggie asked the Guide if the house was haunted. The Guide said, she had heard stories about things moving around and weird sounds, but she hadn't witnessed anything.

The kitchen was in the back of the house. It was amazing; it had everything you could think of for that time. The Guide offered them a cookie and some lemonade, they both said yes. The cookies were really good; the Guide explained that they had found the recipe in an old box they had found in the kitchen, and the cookies are made from the recipe they had found. They think it was the governor's wife, she loved to bake. She handed Aggie some recipe cards, and told her to enjoy. They had decided to share with the people that came to visit the Chickasaw White house. They talked a little more about the history and energy around the property. She told them they could wander around the property if they wanted.

They walked outside, there was a beautiful garden, and it looked like at one time they had a nice orchard. Aggie spotted another Bodark tree, in the field. Aggie told Frank those trees are everywhere, Frank laughed and said you have to wonder way, if you can't eat the fruit, how do they get around? Good question, the birds don't eat them, I guess it would be the wild horses and cattle of the time. According to one of the signs, at one time they had the best peaches and apples in the area. But now there were only a few fruit trees left, and they looked like they had a hard life.

The Guide suggested they should go to the town of Tishomingo, where they are having a Gathering this weekend. There are other historical things to see there too. Just stop by the visitor center and they can tell you about them. They thanked her for the tour, it was getting late and the dogs were home alone, it was time to head back to the RV.

As usual Aggie had to go on line and see what the history of Tishomingo was, this is what she found. "Tishomingo is the Chickasaw Nation's historic capital and heart of the Blue River. Tishomingo was named in honor of the Chickasaw Chief, Tishominko. The City of Tishomingo is rich in history and natural beauty."

"The 1898 Chickasaw Capitol Building and the 1902 Harris Building highlight the historic district along Capitol Avenue. There were two Oklahoma governors, William H."Alfalfa Bill" Murray, and his son, Johnston Murray, that came from Tishomingo. The Pennington Creek flows through the city and into the adjoining National Wildlife Refuge."

After doing a little more research, Aggie suggested to Frank, let's go check the town out this week, Frank agreed. On Thursday they left around 10:00 a.m., after they took the girls for a long walk. When they were getting ready to leave, both of the dogs looked at them and said, GO! We need to rest. Nothing like a long walk to take the wind out of their sails, Frank told Aggie. She smiled and said Yeah, and off they went on another adventure.

Tishomingo, OK wasn't that far only 35 miles away, they went to the visitor center, and the lady there was really helpful. One thing to note if you're going to check out a area, visit the Visitors center or Chamber of Commerce, to find out all the local information. The town was getting ready for the Gathering, the lady at the visitor center told them. It started today, but the festival is on Saturday, and it's something to see.

They thanked her for her help and headed over to the museum across the street, it is the Chickasaw Bank Museum. "It was established in 1902 and served as the official Bank of the Chickasaw Nation until 1906." The front of the building was unusual; it had a large archway with what looked like a fountain on top of it. The building had two floors, and then a bell tower above the door. It was a beautiful stone building, and inside had been restored in the bank area. It was filled with early 1900 furnishings and Native American art work.

After that they walked around the festival area, there a lot of vendors setting up, but that was about it. It looked like they had a lot planned for Saturday. It was too bad they were a day early, Aggie told Frank, he replied Yeah, but we don't like crowds anyway. Let's go have lunch; I saw a Mexican restaurant down the street. Aggie agreed, she was hungry, and Mexican sounded good. It was called

Gonzales, it looked small, but when they went inside, it was a nice size place. The food was great and the prices weren't bad either.

After lunch they walked around the town for a little while, and then headed home. It didn't take long to get there; but they did stop at a liquor store, to pick up something to drink. They found out that they can't sell cold beer; they can only sell warm beer in an Oklahoma liquor store. They weren't sure why, but it was interesting to learn.

When they arrived home, the girls were ready to go for their walk. After the walk, Aggie showed Frank the brochures that she picked up from the visitor center, one of them were about the Chisholm Trail Heritage Center. It's not too far from here, a little over 70 miles; we can stop in Gainesville, and get the oil changed on the Jeep on our way out, Aggie suggested to Frank. She knew how to get him to go on adventure, besides he likes cowboy stuff. Frank agreed with her, and asked When? Aggie suggested a day of rest, and they could go on Thursday. Sounds like a plan, Frank replied.

Aggie figured to push her luck, there some real interesting things to see in Oklahoma City, it's only 130 miles from here as she smiled at him. Frank smiled back at her and replied "Yeah right!" She knew better, it was still hard for Frank to go on long rides, 260 plus in one day was still too much. She was really pushing the 60 mile trip. The Jeep didn't have the best seats anyway.

A day of rest was nice, Aggie wrote in her journal and discovered a large turtle in the pond next to them, it was sun bathing on the bank. It looked to be 10 inches or bigger. Frank worked around the RV, he discovered the tires were low, and there was a leak by the shower. He fixed the leak in no time at all. The tires on the other hand was different, they didn't have an air compressor to fill the tires. After going to the stores in Whitesboro and not fining one, they ended up going Sherman, TX. To make a long story short, three days later, he finally had everything to fill the tires up. It was a very slow process but the tires are now at the right pressure.

During that time they made plans to go to Duncan, Ok to check out Chisholm Trail. Aggie did a little more research about the trail. She had seen a few cowboy movies; the one she remembers most is the one with John Wayne. To her surprise there were at least 27 movies that "had depicted a fictional account of the first drive along the Chisholm Trail."

"The Chisholm Trail was the major route out of Texas for cattle drives. Although it was used only from 1867 to 1884, the longhorn cattle driven north along it provided a steady source of income that helped the impoverished state recover from the Civil War."

"Scot-Cherokee trader Jesse Chisholm first marked the famous Chisholm Trail in 1864 with his wagons. The wagons left ruts in the mud during the raining season, so it was easy to follow the same trail and others to follow him. It started at the convergence of the Little and Big Arkansas River, which went to Jesse Chisholm's Trading post, southwest of present day Oklahoma City."

"Chisholm used the trail to trade with the U.S. Army and Native Americans from his trading post. The Wichita Indians used the Chisholm Trail when they moved from their native territory to the mouth of the Little Arkansas and also when they returned in 1868".

"In 1866, cattle in Texas were worth only $4 per head, compared to over $40 per head in the North and East, because lack of market access during the American Civil War had led to over stock of cattle in Texas. In 1867, Joseph G. McCoy built stockyards in Abilene, Kansas. He encouraged Texas cattlemen to drive their herds to his stockyards. The stockyards shipped 35,000 head that year and became the largest stockyards west of Kansas City, Kansas."

"That same year, O. W. Wheeler answered McCoy's call, and he along with partners used the Chisholm Trail to bring a herd of 2,400 steers from Texas to Abilene. This herd was the first of an estimated 5,000,000 head of Texas cattle to reach Kansas over the Chisholm Trail."

When Frank and Aggie arrived at the Chisholm Trail Center, the first thing they saw was a huge bass display, all were life size. There was a chuck wagon, horses, cattle, cowboys and even a couple of dogs. They went into the museum and where two older ladies welcomed them to the center. It's amazing how many senior citizens volunteer at museums and national parks, Aggie thought to herself. Maybe someday they might do it, but for now they enjoyed exploding this country.

The ladies explained that the Heritage Center has several interactive exhibits including a "4D Theater, animatronics' Jess Chisholm, a reproduction of Duncan's original store, cowboy music, ecology of the trail, and an Art Gallery of the American West."

Jolene one of the ladies at the desk told them, she was getting ready to start the animatronics of Jess at the campfire. They followed her into a room, where another family was waiting. Jolene explained the setting, and gave them a little bit of the history about Jess. Jess was a quiet man and was surprised that the trail was named after him.

Frank and Aggie found a sit; in front of them was a display of two full size men and a full size chuck wagon in a camp setting on stage, with the back ground of the plains of Oklahoma. Then these two animatronics start moving their heads, and talking to each other and from the chuck wagon you could hear the cook and another man yelling. The cook was trying to pull out his bad tooth. It was great, want a great way to learn a little history. The show took about 15 minutes, when it was over Jolene come back and asked Frank and Aggie to follow her to another room.

Once they arrived at the theater room, she explained that it was an interactive movie. She gave some back ground of the story that they were going to see and left again. It was about a cattle drive on the Chisholm Trail. Frank and Aggie were the only ones in the theater so they sat down in the middle of the benches and waited for the movie to start.

The movie started with a scene of cowboys around a campfire, then there was air flowing. At first Aggie assumed it was just the air conditioning, and then as the storm in the movie got stronger, so did the air flow around them. She didn't get the connection in the beginning, then it started raining in the storm, it started raining on them (just a little). Then it hit her, it was the interaction part of the movie. She asked Frank, are you getting wet? He told her yeah! As the weather changed in the movie so did the theater. The interaction made them feel like they were on the cattle drive. There was a stampede in the movie, and the benches they were sitting on started shaking. It felt like they were there, with the wind blowing, water coming down (just a little) and the benches shaking, the loud sounds coming from the movie, it was really well done. After the movie, they both agreed it was pretty cool, and wished they could have shared it with their grandkids.

They walked around the rest of the center, when about fifteen little kids, all 3 to 5 years old, arrived with their mothers. It was fun watching them; looking at the animals, and pushing the button at the different displays. The center has an activities area for kids, for all ages. Aggie asked the ladies up front. They had a few suggestions; they ended up going to Joey place. It wasn't noting to write home about, but the food was good.

After lunch they decided to take another route home. Hwy 81 is part of the old Chisholm Trails, supposedly the area hadn't changed that much, except the trail is now paved and a few more houses. One of the reasons Jess Chisholm took this route is because there was water. Something they had learned at the Center. As Frank and Aggie were going down Hwy 81, they could see why they picked this trail; there were watering hole all along the side of the road.

The next day they started getting ready for the jump to Bay Landing outside of Bridgeport. This is where Frank had heart surgery; they had stayed there for seven weeks. Seven very long weeks as far as Aggie was concern. She was pretty sure Frank felt the same way. They were hoping for a better stay this time.

CHAPTER 16

Back in Bridgeport, TX

The day started out good, the weather was just right and they drove right to Bay Landing, and found a great place to park. It was called the Hollywood section again, because it had all the hook ups. But the last time they were there the power was cut off for a week so they were both hoping that it wouldn't happen again. They hoped to do a little more exploring this time too.

On their second day, they went for a walk around the field; it was a paved road that went around the field. So they didn't have to worry about the stickers in the grass. As they walked along Frank spotted a live snake crawling off into the long grass, he told Aggie it had to be about three foot long. After that Aggie kept the dogs away from the long grass. The maintenance people normally cut the grass back about three feet on both sides of the roads. They continued to walk, when Frank saw another snake; this one was upside down, so of course he had to flip it over. He used his cane; he wanted to see what kind of snake it was. It looked to be about three foot long, but this one was a diamond back rattler. It hasn't been dead very long; in fact it looked like it could be alive. There were no cuts or blood, just some ants crawling on its head. They left it there and continued on their walk. Frank told Aggie; well that was an interesting walk, four deer and two snakes. She had to agree with him.

The next day on their walk, they were looking for the dead snake, and it was gone. Well kind of, at first they didn't see anything, than they saw its rib cage, and then a piece of it skin. It was wild, in one night the snake was gone. Lesson learn don't lay on the side of the road, Aggie told Frank. He had to agree, it was weird everything was gone, except for the two pieces they saw. The head, the rattles which Aggie was kind of hoping to get was gone. The next time they walked by everything was gone.

They had been at Bridgeport for a week, and so far everything had been great. They did road trips, just to check out the area. They went to Weatherford for a recon; they plan on going that way to go to Lake Whitney later in the month.

One thing about Texas there is so many farm roads to travel on. If you miss your turn, just wait for the next road, and turn in the direction you want to go, and you'll find your road again. Most of them are nice two lanes roads, but once and awhile the roads get a little narrow for the RV.

There are old Fort's all over the country; there was one in Jacksboro, not far from the campground. It was called Fort Richardson; it was also a State Park campground. "Fort Richardson was open from 1867-1878, it was home to more than 5000 soldiers and headquarters for Mackenzie's 4th Cavalry regiment. According to the flier, it originally had over 60 buildings, most was only temporary structures and was torn down by locals after the fort was decommissioned."

They arrived at the campground, and found the Fort, there were ten buildings. According to the flier six of the buildings were original buildings. There was the hospital: Morgue, Bakery, Magazine, Commissary and Commanding Officer's Quarters. "The first building was the interpretive center; it was a reproduction of an officer's barracks. It was where the single officer's lived or several families of lesser ranking officers." The Ranger there took them on a tour, with another family that had arrived just before Frank and Aggie got there; they appeared to be grandparents with their grandsons.

First stop the Commanding Officer's quarters, it was another reproduction, but it looked like the real thing. The Ranger said there were five of them at one time, but now it stood alone. It was a huge place, with two large rooms connected by a breeze way. As they were walking around and checking out the rooms, Susan the other woman opened up the closet door, by the entrance way, and screamed. There was a dead body hanging in the closet, well it was a fake body, but it scared Susan and her two grandsons. Frank and Aggie heard the scream, and went back to see what happened. The Ranger said, "It's Halloween anything can happen!" Aggie couldn't stand it she had to look in the closet; sure enough there was a fake hanging body there. She laughed at it and told the Ranger "Good One."

They continued the tour, there was a steel railroad bridge just sitting out in the field, and Frank asked what the deal with the bridge. The Ranger explained the trestle bridge once spanned Lost Creek, back in the steam engine days. The bridge was moved in 1985 to its present location from the bend in the creek, he pointed in the direction of where the creek was. He then said there a funny story about the move of the bridge. He explained, "Each end of the bridge was on two different properties. One of the owners wanted to tear it down and sell the iron, the other wanted to move it onto the Fort's property. The one that wanted to scrap the bridge had to go away on business, and while he was gone the second guy, that wanted to move the bridge to the Fort's property. This was his chance; while the man was gone he had it moved. When the guy came back from his trip, the bridge was gone. But there was nothing he could do about it. The Ranger laughed, there's more than one way to skin a cat!

Next stop the Guardhouse ruins, the Ranger explained "The original Guardhouse consisted of four stone cells, 4 feet by 8 feet. Three soldiers were confined to each cell, if needed. The guardhouse was nearly always at full capacity and additional rooms were added. The post reportedly lost 246 soldiers through desertions."

They continue on the tour to the Enlisted Men's Barracks it was constructed in the picket style. Picket style is logs, with clay and horse manure in between the logs. (It's just clay now) In the winter the mix would stop the cold, and in the summer they would pick out the mix and let the cold air in the evening come through the wall. There was upwards of 150 soldiers crammed in these small building, the living conditions were deplorable. No officer set foot on enlisted row as the stench was so foul."

The next stop the Post Hospital, it was huge. "It was built in 1869 at a cost of $150,000. It consisted of the Dispensary, Post Surgeon's Office, Dining Room, Steward's Room and a Kitchen/Surgery which was attached to the back. There were two wards containing a total of 24 beds." The beds that was on display, had mosquito netting over them; they looked like little cover wagons. In the Dining room they had dishes of fake food, which had huge chunks of meat and a half a plate of beans. The Ranger explained this was pretty much their diet, just beef and beans.

Both Frank and Aggie agreed they could live with that.

The Fort had many interesting things to look at; it took them about two hours to complete the tour. After the tour they checked out the State Park campground next to it. It was very nice, most of the sites had electricity and water, but no septic. After that they went to Jacksboro for lunch, and ate at a pizza place. The pizza was great and the service was great. But it was time to head back to camp.

Halloween was coming up, according to the campground flier. They would have a Halloween Costume party for the kids, and an adult one later that evening. They would bring the kids around on a hay wagon and stopping at each site that was joining in on the fun. Aggie purchased two large bags of candy, thinking that would be more than enough.

They went for their afternoon walk and when they passed the Activities Center. The party for the kids was in full swing, it sounded like they were having a great time. They were surprised to see the place was packed. Aggie turned to Frank and said, I think we're going to need more candy. Frank replied back they are going to need more than one hay wagon! Aggie agreed, let's check with the Ranger and see how many kids they think they will have Trick or treating tonight.

They were walking in the direction of their office, so they stopped there. The Ranger told them; there were over 60 kids at the party. Aggie turned to

Frank, Yeah; we're going to need more candy! Frank just smiled and agreed.

They finished their walk and drove to the Dollar General and picked up three more bags. Now they were ready; they had over 200 piece of candy. Now all they had to do is wait for 4:00 p.m.

The instruction they got from the Ranger was they would pull the hay wagon up to your site, and then they could pass out their candy. The kids would stay on the wagon.

Aggie took their lawn chairs out to the end of the driveway, and saw that the neighbors were doing the same thing. It was funny to look down the road, and see two lawn chairs sitting at each of the sites. It wasn't long before they saw the hay wagons coming down the road. Everyone was in their chairs waiting, Frank told Aggie, I guess they found another wagon, there is two now and it looks like they are full.

When the first wagon pulled up, they walked over to it, and Aggie yelled, "Happy Halloween, I don't hear any trick or treats." The kids and the adults all called back "Trick or treat!" They finished passing out the candy to the first wagon, then the second one came up. This time Aggie called, what do you say? They are replied, "Trick or treat!" she replied "Happy Halloween" and started passing out candy. Then the wagons moved on to the next site.

Frank told Aggie it's going to be a long ride for these kids, there at least 30 more stops. No wonder they started at 4 p.m. Aggie agreed, but it was fun

for us, how much candy do you have left? Frank said
None, I gave it all away. How much do you have,
Aggie said 10 pcs, and good thing we went and got
more candy. They laughed and agreed with her and
said otherwise we might have been mugged.

They had tried to find downtown Decatur a
couple of times, Aggie suggested they try one more
time. She went on line, and thinks she had figured
out what they were doing wrong. Frank agreed, and
suggested they have lunch there, there is supposed to
be a steakhouse in the town square. Aggie smiled and
said, let's go!

They had tried to find downtown Decatur, TX,
a couple of times but they finally found it. As in
most towns downtown seem to be hidden from the
highway. According to the history Aggie found: "The
first known inhabitants in the area were probably
Wichita Indians. When the Coronado Expedition
came through the area of present Decatur in 1540,
there were several Indian villages between the Trinity
and Red rivers. The history of white settlement in
Wise County began with Sam Woody who moved
to Deep Creek in 1854, and his original log cabin
remains as a historic site today."

When they arrived in downtown Decatur, the
courthouse was in the center of the town square. It
was beautiful, and huge, they parked the Jeep and got
out to check it out. It reminded them of a sandstone
building that they have seen in other places. But
according to the flier, "The courthouse materials

used on the exterior include Texas granite in two colors and terra cotta used extensively in the friezes, turrets and dormers." As they walked around the outside, they noticed the art work that was carved into the building was unique. It looked like vines carved in the upper part, with lots of arch ways. It looked more like a castle, than a courthouse. Frank remarked it looks like the castle they made out of sand on the beach.

This was the forth one according to the flier they picked up inside the courthouse. "The third courthouse was destroyed by fire on January 8, 1895. The burning of the third courthouse set off a controversy over the location of the county seat. An election was held in November of 1895 to see if the new courthouse should be constructed at a new location. Voters confirmed by a wide margin that Decatur was to remain the county seat."

The inside was a little disappointing, compared to some of the other courthouses they had visited. It had marble wainscots, stone flooring of contrasting color tiles, and oak doors and trim accent the interior. A winding cast iron staircase in the building's center provides access to the upper floors. Good natural ventilation and lighting are provided by a glass skylight."

When they came out of the courthouse, Aggie smelt steak cooking; sure enough there was a Steakhouse across the street, called Sweetie Pie Steakhouse, they had heard about it. Aggie turned to Frank and said, "Steak time!" He smiled and said, "Of course!" and off they went to eat.

It was a great place, the service was great and the décor was all western. It was lunch time so Aggie only had an 8 oz. steak, it was great, she wished had she ordered a bigger one. Maybe next time, she told Frank, they could come for dinner. After lunch they walked around the town square a little more, then headed back home. It was a nice little area, lots of different places to eat.

They talked to Jr. that night, and he told them that they have found someone to work on their property. He also told them there was more damage than he first told them about. They agreed that they would be down in a week; they had wanted to move to their next site, Texoma.

The cold front had arrived and their furnace wasn't working right. It would come on and light the heater, then it would turn off, and when it came back on it would only blow cold air. It was a good thing they had electric heaters. Aggie always wondered why the heater wasn't like the refrigerator. They could run on either gas or electric. They didn't what to take a chance of freezing the pipes; but they plan on running both electric heaters, instead of the furnace. It wasn't going to get above 30 degrees the whole week; this would be the second week of freezing weather. The water lines in Texoma campground froze so there was no water and the sewer line froze too. What a nightmare that was. Lesson learned, close the sewer lines when there is a freeze coming.

With the cold weather and Aggies tooth killing her they didn't do much, except walk around the campground, and even the walks were pretty quick. Between the cold and the wind, it was in the high 20s during the day.

Aggie gave up and went to the dentist in Whitesboro; she had a bad infection and needed to have her back tooth removed. But they couldn't pull the tooth until the infection was gone. It took a week of antibiotics, but the tooth finally got pulled out. After a few more days she felt much better.

But now it was time to go back to Houston and see the damage from the hurricane. They were missing all the kids anyway. After they got off the phone with Jr., they started talking about what they were going to have to do. Jr. had told them, there wasn't any place to park the RV right now, and everything was a big mess. There is rubbish stacked everywhere; they just got the power on a couple of days ago.

Frank told Jr. they would leave the RV at Lake Tawakoni, outside of Point, TX, and would be down in a couple of days. The next day they set up Penelope on a site by the lake. They were hoping they could come back on the weekends and enjoy the view. It didn't sound like things were going too good down in Houston. According to what they saw on the news and what Frank Jr. had told them.

The campground looked a lot different than the last time. They were here about two years ago. That time the campground was flooded in much of the park, and there was warning's about snakes being driven out by high water. This time there has been a drought here. Where they parked this time it had been under water the last time they were here. They had found a great place to park with a view and not very many people. This is where they met Bella, the campground dog, she was so sweet. Aggie had asked the Ranger about her and she told her that she was dead and explained what happen to her. It was hard to hear that she was dead; they were both looking forward to seeing her.

The next morning they loaded up the girls and headed to Houston. It was going to take about four hours to get to there. They should arrive at Frank Jr. house by 3 p.m. It was going to be a long drive; about 300 miles drive. They were glad that they didn't have to take their RV.

As they got closer to Houston, they could see some of the damages from the hurricane; they could see the flood marks on the walls of the houses, and the walls along the highway.

They pulled into their neighborhood, they saw all of the rubbish from the homes in the area, and many of the houses had construction going on. They pulled onto the road to their house; there were signs of where the trees had fallen. But someone had removed them, the flood waters were gone, but they could tell by the trees that remained standing that they had water marks up to three feet on their trunks. As they turned the corner to see their house, they held their breath; their house didn't look to bad from the outside. There were water marks about two foot high on their stilts. All Frank and Aggie could do is look, and be glad that they had put their house on silts.

They parked the Jeep, and walked around the house and then climbed up the stairs. There was damage inside, according to Frank Jr's. some of the windows were blow out, they had plywood over the broken windows where some water had come in. The floors would have to be removed and some of the walls. All they could do is be thankful they were not there when it happened. They were just glad that the house was still there.

Aggie called Frank Jr. to let him know they were at their house, and would be over in a little bit. He told them he was on his way over there anyway; he had the contractor with him. Aggie said, OK we'll see you in a little bit.

They continued to walk around their house, it looks like four windows, the floor and the walls will have to be repaired. Frank pulled Aggie to him and told her, it's not too bad, at least we had most of our things packed away, and no one got hurt here. Aggie hugged him back; there were no words. Just seeing all of the damage to their house, but the surrounding area was much worse.

After meeting with the contractor and agreeing on the work that needed to be done. They would do the clean up and once they were done the contractor would come in and check the wiring and plumbing and finish the house.

They headed over to Jr's house. His place had gotten hit pretty hard. It looked like half the roof was missing. They both looked at Frank Jr. and asked him, why didn't you tell us how bad your place was hit? He just replied, what would be the point? We didn't what to upset you guys; you have enough on your plate.

All Aggie could do is hug him and told him you should have told us! Where are you and your family staying? Aggie asked him. Jr. told them in a hotel right now, we're trying to find a place to rent until the work is done on our house. Frank suggested, why don't you guys stay in our house, the contractor said he could have it done in a week, once we clean the house out. There's a RV campground not far from here, we'll go get the RV after we get the house cleaned out. We can help out at your place too. After awhile they agreed on a plan. Jr. and family would take their house, and Frank and Aggie would stay at Maria's place, while they were in town.

They drove over to Twila's house, to see how everything was there. It looked like they had a little wind damage, they were higher up. Twilla had told them earlier during the flooding; they could see the neighborhoods that were flooded from their front yard. It was terrible to look down in the valley and see boats instead of cars on the roads below. Twilla showed them some of the pictures she had taken. She told them Dennis and James took their boats down to the flood area and helped pick up people and animals. There were so many pets that people just left behind.

There is still so many people needing help, they have been helping on the weekends. Aggie turned to Frank, let's volunteer, we can work at the food banks, or maybe the animal shelter. Frank agreed, and said once we get set up at Maria's, we'll see what we can do. Twilla asked, does this mean you'll be here for the winter. Aggie smiled and said yes, hopefully we'll go north in April. Twilla gave them a big hug and said; great you'll be here for Christmas.

Aggie turned to Frank, it will seem strange not moving every three weeks; he had to agree with her and replied it'll only be for a couple of months. There is no way you'll be able to sit any longer than three months. Aggie had to agree, she enjoy exploring America.

For the next couple of weeks they helped with clean up and helped at the animal shelter. The first few weeks went by pretty quickly, but Aggie was already getting restless. They decided to go ahead and go back up to Point, and check on Penelope. It's been freezing every night, and staying that way pretty much all day. After the nightmare in Texoma, they didn't what to take any chances.

Jr. and family had settled into their house, and construction was going pretty fast on Jr's. place, it wouldn't be long before they could move back in to their own home. So they packed up their things and headed home to (Penelope). It was great seeing the grandkids, Frank and Aggie was surprised how big they had gotten. They didn't see them as much as they would have liked, between school and their activities, there wasn't much time for them. Sharlene, Tina and Treva would ask Grandpa Frank to teach them how to speak the native language of the Islanders. He had started teaching them when they were little. Frank would just smile and agree. Aggie wasn't sure what language they were talking about. Until later when Frank told her, it's the Merbeing language, I'm even having them communicating under water just in case! Aggie was glad maybe someday they will get to use it, and discover the Merbeings.

The trip back to Point, TX was nice, it was sunny and the traffic was light. When they arrived the dogs acted like they knew where they were at and jumped out of the car and ran to Penelope. It was good to be home. After three years living in Penelope, they had gone through a lot together. They have been in 22 states so far, hopefully after winter, they could explore more states.

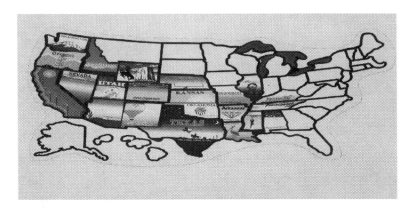

Aggie looked over at Frank and asked him what are you thinking so hard about? Frank relied, "Even though your writing takes up a lot of your time. I was thinking that your book will be a great guide for our kids, and whoever else reads it, when they start traveling." That is if the kids take after us which I believe they will. "That's what I was thinking." "Aggie said, maybe it will keep them from getting lost! They both laughed.

They were looking at the map on the side of Penelope. Aggie told Frank, well we didn't see as many states as we wanted to last year, but we did get 10 new ones. Yea, hopefully starting this spring we'll get a few more states added to the map, and lots more adventures to come. Aggie smiled and went inside their rig.

CHAPTER 17

Hanging out in Texas For The Winter!

I t was great seeing the kids for Christmas, but they had no plan of being in Houston for New Years Eve, because the dogs really hated fireworks. For their next site they are planning to stay at Lake Tawakoni, TX which is outside the town of Point, TX. It isn't too far from Houston, so if they need to go back they could do a day run.

They found a site with a view by the lake, with only a few people around. It was a warm day; it was in the 40's, so it didn't take long to set up camp. The first morning at Lake Tawakoni, they went on a walk, it was in the low 30's, it was a good thing they let the water drip all night. It was a beautiful chilly morning, and there was no wind.

They walked over to the edge of the lake when Aggie looked up and spotted a Bald eagle sitting in a tree. She pointed out the eagle to Frank as she pulled the dogs closer to her. Frank saw what she was doing and said Good idea! The eagle was huge and beautiful, as they continue to watch, it started to fly in their direction. It must have seen the dogs; they are just the right size for an eagle. As it came toward them Aggie pulled the dogs even closer to her. Frank stood in between the eagle and the dogs. The eagle turned and headed out toward the lake, screaming as it went. Aggie told Frank I guess you're a little too big for it. Frank agreed I'm not sure what I would have done if it would have kept coming.

They continued to walk along the water's edge, when they spotted four white pelicans, they were flowing along in the current. Frank told Aggie, I can't believe how many different types of birds they have here. Aggie replied to him, "It's a bird watchers paradise."

It was going to be a cold week, it wasn't going to get above 30 degrees all week, and was going to be pretty windy. This is the type of weather they both could live without. Aggie can't go out in the cold weather, especially when it was windy. It's like she is allergic to it, she starts coughing, and has problems breathing. Frank will take the dogs out for a short walk, when the weather is like this. All they can do is look out the window and watch. But in the afternoon when it finally gets up over 30 degrees, Aggie puts on her scarf around her face, so she can be breath. They both enjoy going for walks in the morning. There was ice on the lake and the grass had little ice bulbs hanging off them, when the sun hit the little bulb's they would glisten.

The ducks are all in large groups on the water, floating together as one unit, there were all types. Frank and Aggie figured that must be how they keep warm at night. Frank laughed and told Aggie, wouldn't it be a hoot if they all started flying with the ice keeping them all together, picking up the water, leaving the bay empty. Aggie responded back, that would be hilarious. What was that movie that we watched the girl told the story about the birds flew away with the Lake. Frank said I think it was "Fried Green Tomatoes." There are enough birds out there to at least take this section of the lake away! Aggie laughed.

After the week of freezing weather, there was a warm day coming up. Aggie and Frank were getting cabin fever again. Aggie suggested they go check out Sulphur Springs, TX. She had heard they had a really interesting courthouse, and a really nice War Memorial dedicated to all branches of the service. It wasn't too far away, so they would be home to take the dogs out for their evening walk. As usual Aggie got on the Internet to find out more about the town. To her surprise it was originally "Founded as Bright

Star in the late 1840s by pioneers who camped and eventually made their home near the more than 100 natural springs that bubbled from the land. They renamed the town in 1871 to Sulphur Springs, and marketed as a health resort due to the healing waters that flowed beneath the surface of the Northeast Texas soil."

"Settlers came in great numbers to benefit from the mineral springs and sulfur baths. In 1872 a railroad line was extended to Mineola, TX. In addition to its medicinal purposes, the self-serve water and fresh water springs allowed crops such as corn and wheat to thrive making the county a local agricultural leader as early as 1860's."

Aggie had been reading this out loud to Frank, and he said, it sounds like an interesting place, but I bet it was a wild place in the late 1800s. Aggie agreed with him. Guess what? Aggie asked. This is another courthouse that had burned down; this is the fourth courthouse that we have been to that had been burned down. "The original courthouse along with the entire east side of the square burned in 1894. The current courthouse made of fireproof, red Texas granite." Well do you want to go tomorrow she asked Frank? He agreed it would be interesting; too bad the mineral springs are not open anymore.

The weather report said it was going to be nice all day, so they headed out around 10 am. It was warmer than it's been in weeks; it was nice to get out of the RV. They had taken the girls out for a long walk before leaving. The girls were running around playing with each other, Frank told Aggie I think they had cabin fever too. I guess, as she tried to pull them along.

They settled the dogs in, and headed out the door. It took about an hour to get Sulphur Springs. As usual downtown was a little ways from the highway. As they drove though the middle of town, it wasn't hard to spot the courthouse. It looked like a red castle, it was beautiful. It had five floors, with a tower on top. Aggie parked the car, and was surprised to hear music playing out of the car. There weren't too many people in the courtyard, so it wasn't coming from them. The music was piped in from speakers build into the courtyard.

They walked around the outside of the courtyard to check it out. They couldn't go in because it was Saturday, so it wasn't open. All they could do is walk around it. Then they walked around the Veterans Memorial. It was really well done. They had all the wars acknowledged and a flag from each of the services. The names of everyone that had died from the county were listed on a wall. It was nice seeing the memorial after so many years. Many of the smaller towns have been putting up some type of war memorial in their towns here in Texas.

The weather was starting to turn, the dark clouds started coming in. They wanted to walk around town a little more but the weather had a different idea. As they headed home, Aggie looked in the rear view mirror, and saw the rain coming down. She told Frank, it's a good thing we left, check out the rain storm behind us. He looked in the side mirror, and replied "Wow, don't stop, it looks like a black wall coming at us. Aggie laughed, and told him, "No kidding!"

The storm headed north and they turned and headed south, where the weather was still sunny. Good old Texas! That evening they watched the local news, they heard that a tornado had touched down in Sulphur Springs. It didn't do too much damage. Aggie told Frank, Man I'm glad we left when we did. Yeah but it would have been kind of cool to see the tornado, Frank replied. Aggie laughed and said yeah it would have been, as long as it was from a distance!

The cold front came back for the next couple of weeks. Jr. had called and said that their house was almost done, and was looking good. It should be done in a couple of weeks. It was good to hear from him, they agreed they would come down when the house was completed.

Well their three weeks at Point was up, they were going back up to Gordonville, TX. It was a clear day, but still in the 30s, they were set up by noon. It's nice to do the short drives, it was only 97 miles. Aggie told Frank, "Welcome back to Lake Texoma! How many times have we been here? Frank said; let's see we were parked,.... After about 1 minute he told her five times. Each time they would park in a different section. This time was no different. The weather was still cold, so every night they would run the water and close the black water tank, because of the last time they were here. Everything had frozen, including the black water. What a nightmare that was, they ended up throwing away the sewage hoses, because it was solid ice, and had to be cut in pieces.

The weather warmed up after a few days, so they decided to go exploring. They wanted to check out a few towns west of them, along the Chisholm Trail. The first stop was Saint Jo; it was the oldest town in Montague County. "Saint Jo was founded in 1849 by Ithane and Prince Singletary who originally called it Head of Elm to its proximity to the headwaters of the Elm Fork. It was an important watering stop for cattle drivers where the Chisholm Trail and the California Road crossed."

"According to some historians, Howell's partner, Captain Irby Holt Boggess named the town after his friend, the "Saint" because Jo was a teetotaler and the Captain was not. Captain Boggess must have thought it took a saintly man to abstain."

The town peaked in 1850; by 2011 it had only grown by 33 people. Aggie told Frank there are five historical makers inside the city: "The First's State Bank, Boggess City Park, the Stonewall Saloon Museum, Phillips Rand and Head of Elm cemetery. There are three Historical cemeteries, including Pioneer, Head of Elm and Mountain Park."

They wandered around the town and it definitely looked like it was built in the 1950s. But because it was winter and a Sunday pretty much everything was closed up. But they did get to eat lunch there, the atmosphere was great and the service was even better. The restaurant was called "Lazy Heart Grill," after lunch they walked around a little bit more and decided to head out towards Bowie. Don from the campground had told them that they had a large bowie knife on display. "It was a new edition to Bowie, Texas it is the world's largest knife, measuring astonishing 20 feet long. The blade itself is 14'5" in length and made purely from steel. This spectacular sight weighs in at 3000 pounds. Good luck fitting this into your pocket.

Settled in the early 1860s, the town, like many in Texas, didn't really get started until the arrival of the railroad. In Bowie's case the year was 1882 and the railroad was the Fort Worth and Denver. In August of that year a town site was laid out and a Post Office applied for. Bowie almost instantly became the most important market and banking center between Fort Worth and Wichita Falls." This came from the brochure they found at Saint Jo about Bowie, Texas. That was enough information to grab Frank and Aggies attention. They had to go to Bridgeport first and get their mail from the PO, and then they would head up to Bowie and check out the knife. It's just a large circle, about 150 miles round trip.

From Saint Jo they took Route 677 South toward Bridgeport, when they discovered "Running N Ranch Art Park." In the middle of nowhere they saw huge metal flowers standing up in the field. They were of assorted colors and even had a leaf on them. As they looked farther across the field there were all kinds of art displays. The one Frank liked the best was the five Volkswagen bugs in a line. Each was red with black dots on it. They were painted up like little ladybugs and they even had legs.

They continued to walk around the field. Well it was more than just a big field; it was an art gallery on steroids. Aggie told Frank this is really cool who would ever think there would be something like this out here in the middle of nowhere. Frank had to agree with her and said it was pretty cool, somebody got bored farming! I guess it's an interesting place. There were no signs to explain who or why it was here. Well it was time to go; Frank told Aggie at least we didn't run into any snakes, just cow patties. True, but it is winter. She smiled, and said I love winters in Texas. It was in the 70's and a clear sky. Next stop Bowie, TX, as they enter Bowie, there stood the Bowie Knife; Aggie pulled over and walked over to it. They weren't kidding when they said it was big. Frank stood by it and Aggie took a picture, just to show how big the knife was. It looked like Frank was just a small dot. It was also used as a Vietnam Memorial. It had listed all the names of the soldiers that had died from the county. There was quite a few of them! There was another couple looking at the knife, and the lady turned to them and said, "I wouldn't what to be around here, if a tornado picked that thing up." Aggie replied, Yeah, but it would be wild to see!

They headed to Bridgeport and picked up the mail at the post office and headed back home. The dogs were really happy to see them needless to say they had to go for their walk. The next few weeks was going to be in the low 30° every night. The next stop was going to be back to Bridgeport, where they would stay for another three weeks and then come back up to Texoma. This is pretty much what they did for the last two months, and would do until April hopefully winter will be over with by then. They wanted to head back to AZ, NM and Utah.

Of course, according to the weather woman this was the worst winter they've had in a long time. They set up the RV by the lake this time and added a few decorations. Aggie had found some metal flowers, hummingbirds and frogs at the dollar store. They only cost a dollar each, so she purchased a dozen of them. She missed planting her flowers and having a garden and this was the next best thing. All she had to do is pull them out of ground and pick them up when they were getting ready to move. It was much easier than having plants! At least she didn't have to bring them into the house when the weather got cold.

A cold front came in after the first week they were in Texoma and it was a cold one, in the high 20s. Every morning there was frost on the car and the trees. They even had snowfall of about an inch at one time. There were icicles hanging off the car and the

RV, it was really strange to see something like that in Texas. Finally the weather broke, so they were able to go for long walks again.

It looks like spring is finally here, look at the blooms on the trees, Aggie told Frank. Frank replied, "Hopefully the cold front that's coming in next week doesn't kill everything." For the next couple of weeks it would be cold in the morning, and warm in the afternoon. They both were ready for spring. It was time to move again, this time to Bay Landing, for three weeks, and hopefully after that heading out to New Mexico. Doug and Dax are coming down for Spring break. Frank and Wanda couldn't come because of work and finishing up their house.

They pick the boys up at 3 am, from the Dallas airport. They were surprise to see how much both of them have grown. After hugs, and small talk they walked to the car.

The weather wasn't all that great while the boys were visiting, so they couldn't go out on the lake. They all went on day trips to Dinosaurs World, and Fort Richardson. While they were at the Fort, an old Cavalry post from the Texas frontier days, two little boys came running up to them. They were about ten and six years old, and told Aggie they saw a soldier outside. Aggie went outside to check it out, there was no one there. They were in the enlisted barracks at the time. She smiled at the boys, and told them I guess it was a ghost. They both looked at each other, and the oldest boy told her, we saw another one in the hospital too. She asked them what was he doing, the youngest boy told her, he was lying on the bed; he had bandages on his head. He just smiled and waved at us, he told her. Aggie asked what did you do, the oldest boy said (like it was no big deal) we waved back. She smiled again and said; well at least he was friendly. Both the boys agreed and continued to follow them around the Fort. They headed over to the hospital, as they entered the hospital the two little boys pointed to the bed they had seen the soldier in earlier. She asked them, is he still there? In unison the boy said, "No!" They wandered around the hospital for a little while, and then went over to the mortuary, which was behind the hospital. There was a wooden coffin set up in the corner. Dax decided that he wanted to get a picture of him inside. Of course, Aggie agreed to it. The youngest little boy that was following them around decided that he wanted to close the coffin with Dax inside. Dax had no objection so the little boy tried to do it. The lid was twice the size of him so his bigger brother helped him. Things that little boys will do! Aggie laughed to herself. As they were getting ready to leave their mother showed up and loaded up the bikes, and left without even saying goodbye.

They drove around the campground and then headed back to the campground. On the way home they stopped at the little store in Run Away Bay Landing and picked up some steaks for dinner. As far as Frank and Aggie were concern they had the best steaks around.

For the next couple of days the weather was cold and windy, but finally there was a sunny day. They all walked over to the pond, which is in the campground, and not far from their RV. They had a bag of bread to feed to the ducks, and the boys wanted to hunt for snakes. There were about 12 to 15 ducks; it didn't take long to go through all the bread. It was crazy to watch; the males would pile onto one female and nearly drown her. They felt like they should do something to help the female but there wasn't much else to do but watch the activity.

There is a large oak tree hanging over the pond. Which Doug decided to climb, there were two main branches, and he went up the left side. He was standing at the end of the branch, when Dax called out "Snake" and pointed to the branch that was going off to the right. Sure enough there was a large snake just lying on the branch. It was hard to spot it at first. Doug went over to check it out; as he was looking at them he spotted there were two little ones lying next to the big one. It was hard to see them, in the beginning, but they raised their heads to see what was going on.

Aggie told Doug, good thing you didn't go to the right; you could have stepped right on them. He agreed and came out of the tree. After that they started looking up in trees. The snakes were Cottonmouth, (aka Water Moccasins). Frank told

Aggie, I guess they wanted to enjoy the sun today too! Aggie agreed and said finally we saw some live snakes after all this year. For the rest of the walk they looked up in the trees. Who knows there may be more, hanging around.

They were sad to see the boys go back home, but at least they had a week with them. After the boys went back home, it was time for Agatha and Frank to get back on the road again. Aggie and Frank we're getting a little antsy, between the weather and the area that they were staying at; there wasn't much else to see. They pretty much had seen everything in the area.

Their plan was to head west in April, there was some family and friends that they wanted to go visit along the way. They also wanted to get out of the Texas heat, this summer. But they still weren't sure where until they got a call from Larie and Dean. Larie told Aggie that they were going overseas for a year and were wondering if they could house sit for them. Larie told Aggie we know how much you and Frank loved Oregon. Aggie looked at Frank and he smiled and said why not, when do you need us there? Larie said, "June would be nice." Great that will give us a couple of months to visit friends and family, Aggie replied. They talked more about the details and then hung up the phone. Aggie smiled at Frank and said, I guess we're spending a year in Oregon. Looks that way, Frank replied.

They started making plans for the trip and called the kids to let them know they are going to Oregon. They all understood, and hoped to come visit them next summer. Frank asked Aggie later, are you planning on keeping a journal while we're in Oregon? Of course, we're not just going to sit around and do nothing. I hear there are all kinds of things to see in the Pacific Northwest! Don't worry about it Frank, there will be a lot more coming, Agatha smiled at Frank. Frank gave her a hug and a kiss, and said I can't imagine you sitting in one place for that long.